IF

YOU'RE

LUCKY

ALSO BY YVONNE PRINZ

The Vinyl Princess
All You Get Is Me

IF YOU'RE LUCKY

YVONNE PRINZ

ALGONQUIN 2015

Published by

Algonquin Young Readers

an imprint of Algonquin Books of Chapel Hill

Post Office Box 2225

Chapel Hill, North Carolina 27515-2225

a division of

Workman Publishing

225 Varick Street

New York, New York 10014

Printed in the United States of America.

Published simultaneously in Canada by Thomas Allen & Son Limited.

Design by Linda McCartney.

LIBRARY OF CONGRESS CATALOGING-IN-PUBLICATION DATA

   Prinz, Yvonne.

   If you're lucky / Yvonne Prinz. — First edition.

        pages cm

   Summary: Determined to clear the fog from her mind in order to uncover
the truth about her brother's death, seventeen-year-old Georgia secretly stops
taking the medication that keeps away the voices in her head.

   ISBN 978-1-61620-463-1

   [1. Mental illness—Fiction. 2. Mystery and detective stories.] I. Title.

   II. Title: If you are lucky.

   PZ7.P93678If 2015

   [Fic]—dc23   2015015879

10 9 8 7 6 5 4 3 2 1

First Edition

For Suzie Neto.
"Long May You Run."

No one who, like me, conjures up the most evil of those half-tamed demons that inhabit the human breast, and seeks to wrestle with them, can expect to come through the struggle unscathed.

—*SIGMUND FREUD,*

Dora: An Analysis of a Case of Hysteria

ONE

The phone rang at four o'clock in the morning. Someone on the other end said that Lucky was dead.

And just like that I was big brotherless.

I didn't cry.

Life without my brother had never even occurred to me. Not once. Sure, I'd become accustomed to little pieces of him disappearing: the tip of his finger to a rock-climbing rope; a chunk of his calf to a baby shark; a front tooth to a ski slope. Lucky's body was a road map of scars. Even his face was covered in nicks and healed-over cuts and faint pinkish railroad tracks from long-gone stitches. That was all fine with me, exciting even, because to me he was indestructible, and because he always came home eventually with more stories and more scars. He always came home until now.

The day before the phone call, I was thinking about how every Christmas I would put a fresh box of Band-Aids in his stocking. He always laughed on Christmas morning when he tore the wrapping paper off the little box. I got him Simpsons Band-Aids one year and Scooby-Doo another; Popeye; Cowboys; Spider Man. There was already a box of Flintstones Band-Aids stashed away in my closet for the coming Christmas and I know just what he would say if he were around to open it: "*Yabba, dabba, doo!*" and then he'd toss it on the pile with the rest of the gear Santa would always bring him. That's how it was: Lucky got gear. I got books. I went digging through Lucky's things that day, the day we got the news, and I found seven unused boxes of Band-Aids lined up in a neat row in a shoebox under his bed. I still didn't cry.

My own scars are different. My body is a desert of soft white skin embellished with small smoothed-over cuts and tears and burns. I don't remember how all of them got there, but the ones I do remember make me wince with embarrassment. I'm the opposite of Lucky. I was born without the thrill-seeking gene. I stick close to home. Heights make me dizzy; the ocean, in my mind, can't be trusted; I despise polar fleece, and I can't see a thing without my contacts in. Some might think Lucky would have been the one my parents worried about, but that wasn't the case. They never seemed to worry about him. It's always been me. Even now, years later, they still look at me with worry in their eyes.

Lucky, on the other hand, had an effortless star quality that made my parents want to be near him. My mom laughed like a teenager when he was around and my dad started making ambitious plans again. There was always stuff everywhere when Lucky was home: camping gear, surfboards, bikes, skateboards, wet suits hanging on the line. There was a happy buzz in our house. Anyone could see that Lucky was my mom and dad's favorite, and I didn't even mind. He was my favorite too. My brother squeezed his big world into our tiny house and made everything seem more exciting, but for me it was more than that. The thing I loved most about Lucky was that he made me feel normal.

Lucky never had much regard for time zones, and besides, it was understood that no matter what time it was or where he was, he should call if there was trouble. The phone ringing in the dead of night was a pretty common occurrence at our house. This time it was different though. Through the wall I could hear the muffled sound of my mom answering, alert even though she'd been asleep for hours. I heard her say "No No No" and then I heard her shake my dad awake. I knew it was bad. She'd never done that before. My dad has to be at the oyster farm by seven.

"My baby!" my mom wailed. The sound was horrible. My heart thumped in my chest but I was paralyzed. I stayed there in my bed, listening.

I heard my dad take the phone. "What is it? What's happened?" he asked.

Lucky had drowned while surfing in Australia at a place called Kirra Beach in Coolangatta in Queensland. I heard my dad talking to them, getting all the details. Then he hung up the phone and started to sob.

Lucky was twenty-two when he died. I'd known him for seventeen years.

TWO

"Fog's staying late today," my dad observed, peering up through the windshield at the gray mid-morning sky as we drove inland in his pickup. I hadn't noticed, but the sky held no hint of summer, which was just around the corner. You get used to that here. From May to September it's like living in a grainy black-and-white film. And it was anybody's guess what time the fog would lose its battle to blue sky and the sun would appear. Some days it didn't appear at all.

We were driving to Santa Rosa to identify Lucky's body, which had made the long journey home to California from Australia by plane. *Where do they put the dead bodies on a plane?* I wondered. I've never seen a coffin bumping along on the airport baggage carousel. They said *identify the body* but of course it was him.

It wasn't like I was clinging to any hope of mistaken identity. I knew it was just a formality, but when Dad asked me to go with him I immediately said yes. Lucky would have gone if it was me, and it should have been me. I'd imagined hundreds of ways that it could have been me and not one where it could have been Lucky. I needed to go.

We passed by the Heron Inn on the way out of town. Miles stood on the deep wooden porch, talking on a cell phone. Miles and Jeff, a couple from San Francisco, run the Inn. They bought it seven years ago and gave it an extreme makeover, painting almost everything a pale shade of buttercream with white trim. They hired Marc, a rock-star chef from the city, and they opened a gourmet restaurant that features local produce, artisanal cheeses, and grass-fed beef. They hired me to make their desserts. I'm good with pastry and I work cheap. Miles waved somberly when he saw my dad's truck. News of the tragedy had no doubt spread like wildfire to every one of the four hundred and eleven residents of False Bay, the hamlet where we live on the coast of Northern California.

Across the road from the Inn, Ralph walked along the shoulder. His droopy-faced bloodhound, Boris, trotted alongside him. Ralph wore black rubber boots and mechanic's overalls. He owns the only gas station in town. He looked over his shoulder and waved as we passed. My dad lifted two fingers off the wheel.

I stared straight ahead at a tiny plastic surfer adhered to the dusty dashboard. Lucky stuck it there ages ago. It bounced back and forth on a little spring, riding endless waves as the truck bumped along. My dad looked over at me a couple of times, but I never turned my head except to glance out my window at a wrecked car on the side of the road. Weeds had overtaken the twisted metal and the rusted exposed engine. It had already been stripped of anything valuable, but at the last second I saw a shoe, a ladies' black patent-leather pump, on the driver's seat. It seemed to be in perfect condition.

When we'd left the house, my mom was still lying on the wooden floor in Lucky's bedroom with one of his T-shirts draped over her face. Rocket, Lucky's dog, lay next to her. The knowing look in his eyes said everything. Rocket hadn't left my mom's side since she went in there shortly after the phone call came. A glass of water sat next to her on the floor untouched. She shouted out words from time to time but mostly she cried out like an animal in pain. I'd had enough of it. I couldn't take it anymore. I put my headphones on and listened to the Clash. I put a rolled-up yoga mat and a blanket next to her. Her long hair was splayed out on the floor around her head, and her eyes were focused on the ceiling. Her feet were bare and blue with cold.

As we drove inland my dad struggled for things to say. Eventually he gave up and fiddled with the radio. He found music but it was sad. Then he found the news. A reporter spoke about a river that had swelled over its banks after days of rain somewhere in Alabama. Several families had been overtaken in the night when river water rushed into their house. All of them had drowned.

"It was their own fault," I finally said.

"What's that?"

"Those people. How could they go to bed with water rising all around them?"

My dad turned the radio off.

Lucky would never have done anything so stupid. He lived to take risks but he knew all about danger. He'd studied it till he was an expert. He knew about tide charts and compasses and wind direction and rogue waves and offshore currents and avalanches and riptides. He knew all of that stuff. So how does a guy like that drown? Why didn't someone save him? Lucky had a million friends. Where was everyone?

A man in a white lab coat with a defeated demeanor and eyebrows like black caterpillars led us to a cold room lit with flickering florescent lights. Lucky was laying on a metal table with a white sheet draped over him. My dad and I stood on either side of him. He looked as calm as I'd ever seen him. His stillness was more disturbing to me than anything. Lucky lived in a constant state of motion. He never slept much but he never seemed tired. Sleep was a waste of time for him. He went to bed late and got up early. He embraced all those tired bumper sticker slogans: *Make today amazing, smile and let it go, life is a highway, BE where you ARE . . . . blah, blah, blah.* I'm nothing like that. I take refuge in sleep. Sometimes I sleep ten hours at a stretch. For me, sleep is a place to hide.

There was a greenish raised bruise on Lucky's forehead with a jagged crimson line running through it, probably from his surfboard. His old scars had taken on a purplish hue and stood out more than before against his pale skin, especially the one on his chin, stitches from I don't remember what fall. I noticed that the thin black cord that he always wore around his neck with the silver charm that said "Fearlessness" in Sanskrit was gone. I wondered if maybe it was in an official manila envelope with his diving watch and anything else they found on the body. Maybe they handed it to you like on TV. *Here's what's left of a life,* the man in the lab coat would say solemnly.

Looking at Lucky, I thought of all the times I'd

said to him, "I wish you were dead." I said it so often that it meant nothing to him. He'd never said anything so mean to me, even when I went crazy and did awful things, even when I ruined birthday parties and family dinners and vacations.

My dad left the room before I did. He was pale and shaking. He sat on the wooden bench in the corridor with his face in his big weathered hands. I could see him through the window in the viewing room.

"Lucky," I whispered, bringing my face close to his until a sour chemical smell burned my nostrils. "Lucky, wake up." I ran my finger through one of his sun-bleached blond curls and then I touched his lips. They felt like cool paper. If he were alive he'd for sure have bitten my finger. Anger washed over me. I resented being left behind. I was always the one left behind. How many times had I said good-bye to my brother? Hundreds, probably. The thing that bugged me the most was that I knew I wasn't enough. I could already feel the gaping hole he'd left that I couldn't even begin to fill. And what about me? How would I cope without Lucky to hide behind? People here knew that if they said things about me they would have to contend with Lucky eventually. He always came to my rescue. Now what would I do?

"Why'd you have to die, asshole?" I blurted, and

I turned and started to leave but then I couldn't. My last words had to mean something. I tried to think of something to say, maybe something about life's journey or how I would always remember him. It all sounded so trite in my head. I thought maybe I should tell him I'd see him in heaven, but I didn't believe in that, and I was pretty sure he didn't either. Finally I leaned in and whispered "I love you," and then I quickly left the room.

THREE

The day before the party I spent the afternoon making Meyer lemon tarts. The Meyer lemons grow on a tree in our backyard, a miracle really, considering the lack of sunshine. I was glad to be in the kitchen, doing something I knew. Lucky loved my lemon tarts. The pale yellow curd filling came out too puckery, but I hate it when lemon curd is overly sweet. To compensate, I added a touch of sugar to the crust. The sugar made the tarts turn golden in the oven. They came out perfect. I lined them up in even rows on a long sheet of parchment paper. I half expected Lucky to appear and snatch a few like he always did when I baked at home.

"Let's just call it a party," said my mom the day we planned it. "He was too young for a memorial. He would hate that word." She was still in Lucky's room, off the floor and in his bed. She was speaking to us now and making sense, though she spent hours staring into space. She was wearing one of Lucky's T-shirts and my dad's sweatpants. I brought her cups of hot tea and toast with blackberry jam.

That was a week earlier. It was the same day that we scattered Lucky's ashes. We drove to the estuary together and got in my dad's boat. He started the engine and steered up the coast to the spot near Fort Ross where Lucky loved to free dive for abalone. The wind was biting and cold and forced little whitecaps onto the bay. My mom, out of the house for the first time, sat huddled in layers and layers of clothes, gazing out at the horizon. The box filled with Lucky's ashes sat next to her on the seat. When my dad cut the engine, my mom put the box on her lap and held it in her hands for a moment. Then she opened it up and dipped her hand into the gray powder. She took a handful and opened her palm, letting the wind take it from her. She handed the box to my dad. I held Rocket's collar and tried to keep the boat pointed upwind while my dad shook the rest of the ashes overboard into the dark water. The boat kept drifting and we ended up with ashes in our hair and our clothes. We watched the swirling ashes mix with the water and change it to pea soup. I wondered how so much life could amount to a box of ashes and the occasional bone chip. The ashes in my dad's beard and my mom's hair made them look old. Within a few seconds, the boat had drifted far away from the greenish slick. I read Lucky's favorite passage from Jack Kerouac's *On the Road*. Then my dad played "Forever Young" on his harmonica. My mom cried. I felt numb.

My dad started the engine again and we headed home. As we pulled into our driveway my mom proclaimed that we would have a party for Lucky. "Nothing macabre," she said, "a celebration of his life." Then she went right back to Lucky's room and curled up on his bed. My dad and I joined her. Sitting side by side on the bed we planned Lucky's party, among his things, surrounded by his surfing posters taped all over the walls.

The night before the party, Sonia, Lucky's girlfriend, arrived home early from college in Vermont to attend. I watched from the kitchen window as her mom's car pulled into their narrow drive, just down the road from our house. Sonia's flight had arrived late. In the dark she looked dazed and moved gingerly, like she'd been in an accident herself. She took a duffle bag from the trunk and went in the house. I was so relieved to see her. Even like this. We were getting close before she went back to college last August. Sonia was someone I could talk to. I hoped that she would stay for a while.

Lucky's friends started pouring in from all over the world. No one expected such a big crowd and we certainly couldn't accommodate everyone. They filled the nearby campground, building a big fire to congregate around at night and share stories about Lucky. It was a beautiful sight from afar, the fire and all of Lucky's friends milling about. They strung a massive old oak tree with fairy lights and decorated it like a Christmas tree, with memorabilia for ornaments. Photos, ski gloves, socks, jewelry, hacky sacks, flippers, surfboard leashes, CDs, sunglasses, and wine bottles hung in the branches. The big tree drooped under the weight of all the stuff.

Sonia and I drove up there in her mom's car and walked through the campground. "The sister and the girlfriend," I heard them whispering as the crowd parted. Sonia knew some of them from when she went to Australia over Christmas break. They offered us beers and shots and pot. I said no thanks but Sonia accepted everything. She seemed to prefer to stay completely wasted, which made her seem uncharacteristically fragile. She was always quiet but decisive and confident. She could almost keep up with Lucky on a surfboard or a ski slope or the side of a cliff. It took Lucky about ten minutes to fall for her when they met two and a half years ago. Sonia and her mom, a radiologist who works in Santa Rosa, rented a small blue house just below us on the hill above town. Lucky was home that summer, working for my dad, and Sonia was home from college. It only took a week before Lucky was following her around like a puppy. Even with all the girls Lucky met out in the world, he'd fallen madly in love with the one whose bedroom window he could see from his own. They were perfect together.

Later that night, we sat in the idling car outside my house. Sonia definitely shouldn't have been driving, but I don't even have a license. I made stupid small talk.

"So, I guess we'll see you at the party tomorrow." I sighed.

"Oh, yeah. Wow, I feel crappy. I should really go to bed. I'm afraid I won't be able to sleep. Where's the party, again?"

"The Heron." I'd already told her that a few times. Where else would it be?

"Right, of course. I knew that." She turned and looked at me. A tear rolled down her cheek. "How much does this suck, George?"

"Tons."

She swiped at her cheek and nodded.

I got out of the car and went inside. My mom was

busy in the kitchen making a pan of lasagna for the party. Though she still slept in Lucky's bed at night, she was venturing out now, a bit more each day.

"Hi, baby." She smiled wistfully at me. I went and stood next to her. She kissed the top of my head. "How was it?"

"Weird. Good. So many people."

She nodded and went back to her meat sauce. Our finely balanced family routine had been toppled. My mom usually spent the days in her studio, a big, bright room with floor-to-ceiling windows behind the house that my dad built for her. She's an artist. She's kind of famous for her hand-built wood-fired pots. Her world is in her studio. She has an electric kettle out there for endless cups of tea and a stereo that she listens to classical music and jazz on. She has an electric kiln for small loads of work and a big gas one for bigger pieces. Out back there's a kiln for wood firings in a sand pit. Before this happened, we didn't see my mom in the house till dinnertime, and then she was only too happy to talk to another human about their day. Now the studio stood dark and we kept bumping into each other, acting as constant reminders of our collective pain. I hoped that my mom would feel like working again soon. It was hard to see her like this, thin and pale and hunched over, wearing Lucky's clothes, her long, beautiful hair matted and dull instead of swept up into a tidy bun like she usually wore it, with a paintbrush or a pencil poked through it. My dad remained powerless to help. He and I said very little to each other. His world was the oyster farm. My world was less clearly defined.

The party turned out to be unbearably nice. Colorful pots and casserole dishes were laid out on a long wooden table in the dining room at the Heron. Too many people brought baked beans but it didn't matter. Jeff and Miles closed the restaurant and Marc, the Heron's temperamental chef, roasted some turkeys. Our neighbors brought salads and breads and cakes and liquor. There had to be about ten guitars in the room, and Lucky's friends played all his favorite songs until later when a reggae band started up. I sat next to Vince, Lucky's surfing buddy from just up the road. He got me a glass of wine at the bar and another one when I finished it. He didn't know that I'm not supposed to drink because of my meds. The wine warmed me and unclenched my stomach. After the band, it was open mic. Lucky's friends came up and spoke, one by one. Vince had had a few beers by then and he stumbled purposefully up to the stage.

"This is total bullshit," he said loudly into the microphone. "Because, you wanna know why? Because shit like this doesn't happen to guys like Lucky. It happens to assholes that don't know how to read waves. I knew Lucky since we were six, man! Lucky was the one who made us safe on the water. That guy saved *me* so many times I lost count. I totally owe him my life. I don't know how this could have happened to him but it's total bullshit . . . okay?" He stared the crowd down and then he lurched off the stage.

The open mic was the hardest part of the night. Especially when my dad rose slowly, unsteadily from his chair and made his way to the stage, holding a mug of beer. I cringed. I wasn't sure I wanted to hear what he had to say. The room went silent. He stood there a moment, gazing at something off in the distance. Then he cleared his throat and began speaking: "Thank you all for coming. My son . . . you know him as Lucky but he was born Ludwig, named for my grandfather, a stupid name for a boy like that, we soon realized. He was nothing like my grandfather at all. He was . . ."

My dad stopped. He took a deep breath and went on. I couldn't look at him.

"I'm sorry, I'm not accustomed to talking about him in the past tense. Anyway, Lucky had a way of living that made me envious. He was ravenous for life. He couldn't seem to pack enough of it in . . ." He paused. The room waited. "And he was always like that. When he was four, he started coming out on the boat with me and he'd stand up the whole way—he already had his sea legs—and he'd watch the horizon as though he was trying to figure out the fastest way to get there. He'd point to it and say 'Papa, can we go there?'" He paused again and inhaled raggedly and then he seemed to remember something that made him smile.

The crowd waited patiently. He looked out at all of Lucky's rosy-cheeked, dread-locked, tattooed friends.

"And look at all of you. Most of you I've never even met and here you are, some of you came so far. My wife, Madeleine, and I are very, very grateful. It makes us feel better to know that you knew our son too . . . and that you miss him, and that you won't forget him. Thank you."

My dad raised his mug.

"To Lucky."

The crowd raised their glasses: "To Lucky."

My dad returned to his chair next to my mom, draping his arm around her shoulders. She kissed him and he took a folded handkerchief out of his pocket and dabbed her tears. My mom had pulled herself to-gether for the party. She was wearing a long denim skirt and a mohair sweater. I could see her telling my dad she wanted to leave. They got up together and slowly moved toward the entrance of the dining room. People stood up as they passed and my dad shook hands with the men and the women kissed my mom's cheek or they hugged her. My dad squeezed my shoulder as they passed by.

"See you at home," he said.

I scanned the room for Sonia and spotted her at the bar, having a conversation with a guy. He was wearing a T-shirt I thought I remembered Lucky wearing. I wasn't surprised; Lucky always gave his things away. What was his was yours. He had no need for material goods. Sonia seemed to know the guy. She said something to him and he shook his head and looked hurt. Then she hugged him as though she was apologizing. They stayed like that, hugging, for longer than most people hug. I wondered who he was.

Later, I saw the same guy sitting alone at the bar as I made my way to the bathroom. I was dizzy from the wine.

"Hey," he said as I passed him, "you're Georgia, right?"

"Yeah." I slowed. "How'd you know?"

"Are you kidding? You look just like Lucky." He offered his hand. "I'm Fin."

I shook his hand. It felt cool and his fingers were long and thin, like a pianist's. The name sounded vaguely familiar. Lucky had probably mentioned him to me in his many rambling e-mails. He'd talked about so many of his friends. Fin let go of my hand. I reluctantly looked away and glanced around the room. The party guests were drunkenly hanging off each other, hugging and kissing. I looked back at Fin and laughed.

"Lucky would have loved this party," I said.

"Yes. He was the life of every party."

"How well did you know him?"

"Very. I was actually with him, you know, when he . . . had the accident."

"Yeah?" I looked at him with renewed interest.

He nodded solemnly. I wished we could go somewhere quiet and he could tell me everything about the last few minutes of my brother's life.

There were several friends who'd made statements to the Australian police about what happened. Fin probably had too, I couldn't remember. A week earlier the report had been sitting on our kitchen table, and I sat down and read it till the hair on the back of my neck stood up. They said Lucky had wiped out off a big wave. No one else had dared jump on that wave. He was riding it fine but then he seemed to lose his balance slightly. The wave tossed him up and dumped him hard and a massive wall of gnarly water slammed down onto him. Some of his friends said that they thought his board was tombstoning, which can mean that a surfer is trapped in deep water, disoriented, or that his leash could be caught on a rock or some coral. Everyone watched for Lucky's head to pop up but it just didn't. He was under for way too long. Someone, maybe it was Fin, got to the board and dove down into the churning water and found Lucky. He ripped the Velcro band off Lucky's foot and pulled him to the surface but it was too late. Lucky had been hit on the head with his board and he was probably unconscious and unable to free himself. This had all happened in about ten feet of water. For Lucky, that was like drowning in a bathtub.

Fin didn't look like a surfer. He looked more like a South American polo player: olive-skinned with dark, intelligent eyes and a longish, thin nose. His light-brown hair was tangled and fell loosely around his face. There was no sign of the early crow's feet or the permanently sunburned nose or the sea-salt-fried, sun-damaged hair you see on most surfers. He had an intensity in his eyes that was separate from the rest of his face. His mouth turned up at the corners into a slight smile but his eyes expressed something else, something deeper. He also didn't talk like a surfer. Frankly, I'd had enough surfer talk to last me a lifetime. The way Fin spoke was refreshing.

The reggae band had started up again. Fin said something to me I couldn't hear and I leaned in closer. "What?"

His lips brushed against my hair and I felt his warm breath on my ear. The wine had relaxed me and I felt a small current of attraction zip through my belly. He repeated himself. "I said you're beautiful."

I wasn't expecting that. Could he be flirting? I was flattered. I felt myself blushing.

He laughed. "I'm sorry. I didn't mean to embarrass you. It's just that I feel like I know you already. You look so much like Lucky."

"Yes. You said that."

"But different, more delicate, and your eyes are a bit more green than blue. Lucky's eyes were blue."

"He had my dad's eyes. I have my mom's."

I looked down. I noticed he was wearing a black cord around his neck. There was something silver hanging from it, dangling just below his T-shirt collar. I pointed to it.

"What's that?" I asked.

He pulled the silver charm out from below the neck of his T-shirt: Fearlessness, written in Sanskrit.

"It was Lucky's," said Fin, leaning in again.

"I know."

"He gave it to me. When I first met him, I'd just

crashed my motorcycle. I was a bit of a mess. Then I fell off a roof I was working on and then he watched me surf and he figured I needed it more than he did."

"Oh." I was a bit hurt. Lucky had always said that I could have it. That was typical Lucky though; he'd probably given it to Fin without a second thought. I remembered one time, I'd slipped it off Lucky's neck while we were sitting side by side on the sofa, and put it on mine. He angrily demanded I give it back. I remember taking it off my neck and dangling it in front of him, teasing him. He grabbed for it and I yanked it away and stuffed it in my mouth. It tasted salty. He pounced on me, squeezing my cheeks together till I laughed so hard that I spit it out. *It's for luck,* he had said. *You can have it when I'm dead.* And I remember my response too: *If you're dead it's not really working, is it?* I never thought about that charm again until I noticed it was missing from Lucky's neck at the morgue.

Fin studied my face. "Do you want it? You should have it. Here . . ." He started to take it off.

"No. Don't be silly. He gave it to you. You should have something to remember him by."

"That's very kind of you. It means a lot to me." He gestured at the empty barstool next to him. "Why don't you sit down?"

I looked at the empty chair and then back at him. "Did Lucky tell you about me?" I asked.

"No. Sit. Tell me all about you." He smiled.

I could feel my face getting hot again. "I'm sorry. I have to go."

I rushed to the bathroom but someone was using it. I walked quickly down the hallway and out onto the front porch of the Inn where the air was heavy and cool. I took deep breaths. I shook my head at how childishly I'd just behaved, running away from Fin like an overly sensitive little girl. The porch was quiet and I could hear the soft rumble of the surf rolling in. I smelled Marc's peculiar European cigarettes. He sat in the shadows on the porch swing, smoking, still in his chef's whites. Marc is Swiss French and barely civil to anyone, though lately I'd received a few nods of approval from him for my desserts.

"Sorry for your loss," he said, exhaling smoke.

"Thank you."

"Would you like a cigarette?" He expertly shook one out of the pack and offered it to me.

"No. Thanks." I took the wooden porch steps down to the pavement. I crossed the highway and found my way through the darkness to the beach where I sat down in the damp sand and watched the oily black water until I was numb with cold. I heard raised voices and heavy steps on the wooden deck behind me. I looked back at the brightly lit Inn. A girl I was quite sure was Sonia ran across the porch with someone following her.

"You shouldn't have come!" she shouted. It was definitely Sonia.

"Wait!" said a man. He followed her down the stairs to the parking lot. They disappeared into the darkness. I watched the Inn and listened but I heard nothing more except the dull noise from the party. After a few minutes I saw Sonia walk back inside alone. A car passed by on the highway. I turned back to the water.

FOUR

Several weeks had passed since the party for Lucky. Somehow it was already late June. I was starting to tire of the looks the locals kept giving me. I look enough like my brother to light a spark of hope in their eyes. I could almost see them thinking, *Lucky?* And then remembering, *Oh, right, Lucky's dead, it's just George.* They didn't mean any harm by it, but couldn't they tell by my face that I missed him so much it hurt?

I was reluctantly back in the work groove at my other job at Katy's Kites and Salt Water Taffy, which opened at ten sharp on Saturday mornings. The sharp part is because Katy, the owner, who lives in Petaluma, likes to call every morning, even though the place never gets customers for the first hour. Once she knows the store is up and running, she can go back to her gifted twins' soccer games and ballet recitals. At 9:55, I unlocked the front door, turned off the alarm, flicked on the neon OPEN sign, and went outside where I hung several long-tailed kites from their hooks under the eaves to flap around in the wind all day. No one really buys kites anymore. People come for the taffy. The phone started ringing right on time and I ran inside to answer it.

"Hi, Katy."

"Hi, Georgia. Everything okay? Have you restocked the bins?"

"Yes," I lied. "Everything's great."

The fog was thinning. Big puzzle pieces of blue were appearing through the gray. It would most likely be sunny by early afternoon. I restocked the taffy bins. Katy's features thirty-five flavors. I used to like how some of the flavors, like lemonade or apple pie, would evoke happy memories of my childhood with Lucky, but I've come to hate all of them. The flavors are all fake. The thought of a whole summer of this made me feel weary, but I needed the job.

Sharona, my part-time coworker, arrived late, full of the usual apologies and hung over, the remnants of last night's makeup blurring her pretty features. She smelled like liquor and cigarettes. Sharona and I are only three months apart in age but there is little evidence to suggest that. For instance: She already owns her own car, a rusted-out Toyota wagon she's been driving since the minute she turned sixteen. She knows how to get a fake ID and how to get cheap concert tickets online and how to apply smoky eye makeup. She knows how to buy lingerie and where to get a good tattoo and how to get to San Quentin to visit her dad every month. He got into some sort of trouble years ago but he found religion in jail. Sharona went the same way when her home life started to fall apart and she believes that God has forgiven her dad. She told me that they read the Bible together when she visits. The thing I like best about Sharona is that she never judges anyone. We get along great and she's one of the few people in town who really knows me and still treats me like I'm normal.

I handed her a latte in a to-go cup. Lattes are part of my Saturday ritual. Before work I always stop by the Heron and pick up one for each of us.

"It might even still be hot," I said.

"Mmmmm." She smiled and sipped it gratefully. "Hi, by the way."

"Hi."

I counted out the change drawer while Sharona straightened up the bins of taffy. The smell in this place, a sweet artificial berry smell, is sickening so early in the day. I pulled my wool turtleneck up over my nose. All of my clothes smell like this place.

Sharona's not a fan of dead air. She likes to chatter away while she works but I don't mind. I like listening to her. I watched her wince as she bent over the lowest row of bins. A small gold crucifix dangled between her breasts, bouncing off a tattoo of a coiled cobra.

"Man, I feel awful," she said, standing up straight, arching her back.

"What did you do last night?" I asked.

"Mags and I were at the laundromat because my mom's washing machine broke again and we met this guy there who was on his way to a party in Santa Rosa so we went with him. It was off the hook. I think it was the Jell-O shots that did me in. . . ." She paused and a look of alarm spread across her face. "Damn!"

She ran over to her purse at the checkout, digging through it till she found her phone. "Damn!" she said again as she punched in a number and looked at me, shaking her head, tapping her foot.

"Hey, Mags, it's me. Did you happen to pick up the laundry last night? 'Cause I didn't. Please say you did. Call me." She clicked off her phone. "Oh, man. I hope she remembered. We left our stuff in the dryer. I am such an idiot."

She dropped her phone into her bag. That's another thing about Sharona: She carries a purse, not a backpack, and it's full of things like car keys and lipstick and cigarettes and birth control.

Sharona pulled the phone book out of the drawer and started thumbing through it. "What's the name of that laundromat again?" she asked quietly, running her finger up and down a page. "It's Mister Soapy or Mister Sudsy or something. . . ."

She wasn't really talking to me. There is a velocity to Sharona that is more spectator sport than interactive. I gazed out the window, preoccupied. I'd been thinking about Sonia all morning. It kind of surprised me that she was still here in False Bay. I would have thought she'd have gone back to school by now. She had to have missed her final exams. Maybe she didn't care. Anyway, I wasn't one to talk. I'd worked the pity angle with my teachers in most of my classes. Easy enough. I've always been known as the "fragile" girl at school. Based on my colorful history, no one wanted to see how I dealt with the death of my brother. Some of my teachers made me write the final at home, and some of them just gave me a passing grade, but I never went back to class after Lucky died. Maybe Sonia would stay on for the summer. Maybe she could get a job around here somewhere. I could even help her find one. We hadn't hung out as much as I'd have liked. I thought we'd be a comfort to each other but she'd been spending her days alone at home.

The bell on the door tinkled. Our first customers of the day, a woman and two kids. The kids bolted for the taffy bins. They'd obviously been offered it as a reward for good behavior. On the weekends, a caravan of SUVs filled with families from the city passes through town on their way to Sea Ranch for the weekend. The younger couples go to Mendocino for romantic getaways with wine tastings and hot tubs.

The kids knew the drill. They greedily filled a plastic bag.

"*No* peanut butter!" commanded the little girl, watching her brother bury his arm in the bin.

He looked at her defiantly and dropped a handful of peanut butter taffy into the bag. She pinched his arm hard enough to leave a bruise. I was shocked at the anger in her eyes as she did it. Her brother yanked his arm back and started wailing.

"Retard," she said, thrusting her chin out at him.

I looked at the mom but she was texting on a phone that she'd just pulled from her oversized leather handbag.

"Mom!" shrieked the little boy.

"What?" said the woman, eyes still on her phone, thumbs tapping away.

The little boy charged at his sister, kicking her in the shin. Now she was wailing too. Sharona and I exchanged a look. I felt a pang of sadness. Lucky was so generous with me when I was that age. At the first quivering of my lower lip he would grab me and turn me upside down or spin me around till I shrieked with laughter. There was no venom between us. We weren't like these kids.

The truth is, I don't have the stamina for retail. I can barely muster up a smile, let alone be civil to the weekenders. To me, they're all interlopers. Sharona, on the other hand, is endlessly patient with them. She stepped in and refereed the kids, cheerfully helping them fill their bag until the mom checked back in, digging through her bottomless handbag and producing a wallet. They finally left and I exhaled. Sharona picked up a few pieces of stray taffy off the carpet and went back to her chatter.

Out the window I saw a car pull up. Two girls, about the same age as Sharona and me, walked across the parking lot. A boy waited in the car, looking moody, staring at his phone. The girls quickly filled a bag. They paid and got themselves back in the car. The kid burned rubber out of the parking lot. City kids always like to let you know that they have somewhere more important to be.

Toward the end of last summer I met a city kid named Ryan. He was staying at his parents' ocean-front vacation home, which was three times the size of my house. I guess I knew he was all wrong for me. I knew that he thought of me as a "townie," exotic only because I was a country he hadn't conquered yet. I didn't care about that. I liked him. He was new and he was bold. I liked the way he threw his strong arm around me and pulled me close whenever we walked anywhere. He had loads of confidence. He was posses-sive. He wanted me to know that I belonged to him.

I was a virgin and I wanted to have sex with someone who didn't know about my past, someone who didn't think I was crazy. When I told him it was my first time I thought he would be gentle with me and take it slow, but he unceremoniously swiped my virginity in the back of his dad's new Escalade. I left a bloodstain on the beige upholstery. "Shit! My dad's gonna kill me," he said. I got most of it out with cold water, but I felt bad and embarrassed about the stain and I felt worse about the fact that I'd had sex for the first time with someone who cared about things like upholstery more than he cared about me.

I didn't hear from Ryan again after that. Hav-ing sex with him had summoned up emotions in me I hadn't expected. I needed to talk to him. I called a few times but he never picked up or returned my calls. I saw him a couple of weeks ago at the grocery store, trying to buy beer with a thin wisp of girl in tow. Kara, at the checkout, was not going for it. She told them, *No ID, no beer.* I stayed hidden in the cracker section. Ryan stalked out of the store with the girl trailing behind. I heard her call him "baby" as she tried to console him. If Ryan were a local he'd have known that Clive, who works at Ralph's gas station, will buy beer for anyone who pays him five bucks.

As the day wore on, the constant jingling of the bell on the door started my head pounding. The headaches were back. They were caused by the meds Dr. Saul prescribed six months ago. The meds he had me on before these made me feel morose and sometimes made me think about killing myself, so Dr. Saul switched me to these. He told me that the headaches would go away soon. He said that three months ago.

Sharona noticed. Even when she's nursing a hangover, Sharona is thoughtful.

"You okay? You look peaked. Is your head hurting again?"

"A bit."

She came around behind me and gently massaged the tight tendons in my neck with her thumbs. I inhaled her mint gum and her perfume oil, a blend of patchouli and vanilla. Her hands were warm and soft and I didn't care that they smelled like cigarettes.

"Relax," she said.

I tried to.

"When's your next appointment with Dr. Frankenstein?" she asked.

"Um, next week, I think."

"You should get off these meds. They suck."

"Mmmmm." I didn't want to get into how complicated it all was. I just wanted to enjoy her hands rubbing my tight muscles.

"Oh, I can't believe I forgot to tell you this. I met this guy last night, and he works at that casino in Graton, parking cars. He says that the tips are amazing: two hundred bucks a night sometimes. If people win they throw him a twenty just for getting their car. He's going to talk to his boss and try and get me an interview."

"You'd quit this job?" I couldn't imagine working here without Sharona.

"Hell, yes." She paused, realizing how that sounded. "'Cause, you know, I just need to make a lot more money. I mean, it's not a sure thing or anything like that. It's just . . . Anyway, he was drinking. . . . He probably forgot."

"No he didn't."

"We'll see. Does that feel better?"

"Yes. Much. Thanks."

"Sure." She squeezed my shoulders.

The fog disappeared from the sky and a steady stream of optimistic weekenders came and went. I weighed a bag of taffy for a couple.

"We are *so* bad," the girl in tight jeans kept saying. "I'm going to be on the treadmill *all* weekend after this." Her voice sounded like a squeak toy and she had a wide, bland face that was out of proportion with her wiry, toned body. I had to look away or I'd have said something rude. Out the window, I saw a guy pedaling along the highway on a weathered old bike. He wore a newsboy cap backward on his head and he had the unmistakable ease of a local: no bells and whistles on his bike, nothing slick about his clothes. I was sure I'd seen him somewhere before, but I couldn't think where. He stopped pedaling and coasted past Sharona, who was smoking on the porch. He said something to her and she touched her hair as she responded. He nodded and gave her a friendly wave as he pedaled away.

"Four-fifty." I said to the couple. The guy gave me a credit card. *Really?*

I handed the bag to the skinny girl and walked out onto the porch as the bicyclist slowly disappeared around the bend in the highway. He seemed to be in no particular hurry.

"Who was that?"

"I'm not sure. He's cute." Sharona stepped on her cigarette butt and kicked it off the porch with the toe of her boot.

We stood there a moment. The couple headed back to their Porsche. They were undoubtedly on their way to a cramped B and B in Mendocino featuring calico quilts and a four p.m. complimentary wine and cheese tasting. I waved absently to them. I was still trying to figure out where I'd seen that guy before.

FIVE

Early Sunday morning in the kitchen at the Heron, I started on my first ever batch of lavender shortbread cookies. Jeff and Miles had recently returned from a trip to the city where a restaurant they dined at featured a cookie plate on the dessert menu. Jeff described it as "a divine assortment of tiny, exquisite cookies that sent him straight to heaven." Anyway, not to be outdone, the Heron will now feature one on its dessert menu; nine dollars for a few cookies on a plate, with an edible flower for garnish (because the little cookies aren't pretentious enough). We finally settled on lavender shortbread, tiny coconut meringues, and an espresso-chocolate-mint sandwich.

I unwrapped the cold butter and dropped it into the industrial mixer on the stainless-steel prep table. It made a satisfying thud as it hit the bottom of the big metal bowl. That's when I spied him again. I happened to glance out the pass-through window where the waiters pick up plates of food. Jeff and Miles were sitting at a table in the dining room working on their bills and staff schedules, as they do every Sunday morning, and he sauntered in. No hat. It was the hat that threw me off the day before. The guy was Fin, Lucky's friend from the party. *What's he doing here?* I wondered. The party was weeks ago. Hadn't he said that he lived far away? Or had he? Actually, now that I thought about it, I couldn't remember him saying anything about living anywhere.

Jeff and Miles both shook his hand and looked happy to see him. I mean, *really* happy. He sat down at the table. I turned off the mixer, took out my iPod earbuds, and stood at the pass-through, watching. Karl, the short-order breakfast cook, walked over from the griddle and stood next to me.

"Who's that?" he asked.

"Fin."

"Well, he better not be after my job 'cause. . . ."

"No one wants your job, Karl."

"Just sayin'." He went back to the griddle, grumbling to himself.

Karl is only a year older than I am. He's a little

overprotective of his job here. Karl and Sharona dated for awhile. He tattooed her name onto his bicep and had to have it lasered off when she broke up with him. You can still sort of see it. Sharona stays away when Karl is working. I don't mind Karl. His country potatoes with fresh rosemary are transporting.

I smoothed my apron, grabbed a clean mug and a full coffee pot off the warmer, and walked out into the dining room, trying to look super casual. Fin's eyes met mine and there was no doubt that he knew who I was. He even looked as though he might have been expecting me.

"Georgia, hi."

"Hi." I gestured with the coffee pot and he nodded.

"Sure. Thanks."

I filled the mug and then I refilled Miles's and Jeff's mugs too. They looked surprised. Serving coffee is not part of my job description, but then neither is removing a dead rat from a trap in the pantry and somehow I always end up doing it.

Once all three mugs were filled, there was really no reason for me to be standing there. I hadn't thought this through. A few awkward seconds passed where all three of them looked at me expectantly.

"Okay, then," I said and I walked away, carrying

the pot. I risked a look back over my shoulder. Fin was watching me.

Back in the kitchen, I observed him from my vantage point at the pass-through. His eyes were lively and expressive and his mouth stayed curved into that slight smile I remembered from the party. It was as though he were amused by life. The way he used his hands a lot when he spoke made him look like a foreigner. I could see Miles reacting to him too, leaning in, laughing. I knew Jeff would accuse him of flirting later.

I was intrigued by this Fin person. I needed to know more about him. For just a second, I wanted to run home and e-mail Lucky and ask him who this guy was, but then I remembered that I can't. Lately, I'd been managing better. I sometimes went five full minutes where I didn't think about Lucky. And when I woke up in the morning, there were those few seconds where my mind was free of the heaviness, but then it always came rushing back to me. I had dreams about water pressing down on me and I'm panicking, trying to get air. Lucky is calling for help. I can see him but all the waving of my arms and legs doesn't get me any nearer to him in the murky water. I wake up gasping in the dark.

I went back to my shortbread, adding the sugar and creaming the butter till it lightened up to a pale yellow. I added the dried lavender and mint and watched it disappear into the butter, turning the mixture fragrant. I sifted in the dry ingredients and turned the mixer off when it formed a dough. I put my earbuds back in and lost myself to *Sticky Fingers* by the Stones. Suddenly Fin was standing right in front of me. I looked up and jumped, startled. He smiled and I pulled out my buds again.

"Hey, Georgia. Sorry, didn't mean to scare you." He was wearing a weathered old suede jacket and his hands were shoved into the front pockets of his jeans.

"Uh, that's okay." I smiled. "You can call me George. Most people do."

"Okay, then I will too, from now on. Jeff and Miles just hired me. I'm waiting tables here a couple nights a week so I guess we'll be seeing a lot of each other."

I was confused. "You'll be working here?" I wiped my hands on my apron.

"Yeah." He looked around the kitchen.

"Why?"

"I've decided to stay on here. Lucky always talked about this place like it was something special, and now that I've seen it for myself I know what he meant."

I smiled. "Really? Special?"

He nodded. "I love it here. Don't you?"

Did I? I wasn't sure. Right now I felt anchored to it, but it wasn't because I loved it; it was more because I was afraid to leave. I had a stack of abandoned, half-filled-out college applications in my desk drawer at home. I'd gotten as far as the first essay question: *How have you grown or developed over the last five years?* How had I? Had I? I'd only started filling them out because everyone at my high school was doing it. I had a different plan, though, a secret plan for the future that I'd shared with no one. I was stashing any money I could from my two jobs into a slowly growing bank account. My hope was that I could eventually apply for a scholarship to attend the Culinary Institute of America in St. Helena. They offered a two-year certificate program in the Baking and Pastry Arts. I'd immediately liked the sound of that when I started reading about it online. The campus was not that far from here. The main building was a massive stone castle called Greystone. I'd pored over the photos on the website of all the eager young students in their crisp chef's whites learning at the elbow of famous chefs and I imagined myself there with them, learning to make a perfect brûlée or a crème anglaise or a *pâte a choux.* But now that Lucky was dead, all the air had gone out of my plan. It felt like a fantasy, something someone like me could only dream about.

Still, if I left this place, I could start over as a girl named Georgia instead of George, Lucky's crazy sister. Maybe that's why Fin was here, maybe *he* was starting over.

"Sure," I said, "I guess I like it here okay. It's not for everyone though. You've probably noticed that summer never really arrives and it's kind of . . . minimal and gloomy." I looked out the window at the morning fog. "This is pretty much it for the next three months."

"I adore gloomy." He grinned.

"Me too."

"So we have that in common." His eyes lingered on mine. He was so confident. It unnerved me. I'm drawn to confidence like a moth to a lightbulb. I'm in awe of people who are good at life.

"You do look so much like Lucky, you know."

"I know." I winced. He caught it.

"Oh, jeez. I'm sorry. I didn't mean to . . ."

Did he have a slight accent? There was something subtle, off in the background, but I couldn't be sure.

"Don't worry about it. It's okay."

Again he lingered on my face. "Maybe you and I could get a coffee sometime, get to know each other a little better. I have to confess, when I look at your face, I sort of feel like I know you already."

I wished so much that I could be the person he thought he knew. I was nothing like Lucky.

"Sure. I'd like that. Whenever."

"Great." He reached out and took a strand of my hair between his fingers.

"You've got a bit of dough . . . here, got it." He wiped it on his pants. Something about the way he did it seemed very intimate to me.

"Well, I'd better go get my apron and then Jeff wants to show me his Japanese woodcut prints. I'll see you later, George."

"Yeah, sure."

That was the first I'd heard about Jeff's Japanese woodcut prints.

Fin disappeared through the swinging kitchen door.

I sliced silver-dollar-sized cookies onto the cookie sheet. Was it strange that Fin had suddenly arrived here? False Bay wasn't really an adventure destination. Lucky had always left this place in search of excitement. He became restless if he stayed home too long. I wondered if Fin realized just how sleepy this town could be.

I started on a new batch of cookies and quietly sang along to "Dead Flowers" on my iPod.

SIX

A noisy pickup truck pulled up alongside me. I walked a few steps before I stopped and turned around. I already knew it was Fin. The truck looked old and it had Oregon plates. Fin waved from behind the wheel and I walked around to the driver's side.

"You can't be lost."

"I'm not." He grinned. "You need a ride home?"

"No. Not really. I live right up this hill." I pointed.

"How about just a ride then?"

"Where to?" I asked. *Who cares?* I thought.

"I don't know. Come on. Hop in."

So I did. I think I might have jumped in even if he said he was driving back to Oregon. There was just something about him. Maybe it was that same ease that Lucky had in the world. I was always happiest

driving next to Lucky, even if we weren't going anywhere in particular.

Fin turned right on the Coast Highway and we
headed north.

I showed him how to get to my own private beach
about five miles down the road. Hardly anyone ever
went there. It was hard to find if you didn't know your
way. Fin parked the truck on a gravel pullout and we
hiked down the steep path of switchbacks to a small
sandy cove surrounded on two sides by sheer rocky
cliffs.

I kicked off my shoes, but Fin kept his boots
on as we walked across the smooth, dark sand. The
beach was windy and the sand was damp but we sat
down next to each other and looked out at the waves.
I hugged my knees. I hated that I was wearing my work
clothes. I smelled like food.

"Technically, this is Lucky's beach. He found it
first," I said.

"You must really miss him." He looked at me.

I didn't say anything.

"I know *I* do. But I can almost feel him here. It's
almost like he's still alive when I'm here, you know?"

"Is that why you came?"

"No." He looked up at the fog hanging off the
coast. "I came for the weather."

I smiled. "Very funny. I forget, did you tell me how you met Lucky?"

"We didn't really meet. We just ended up in all the same places and we got to talking. Before long we were like brothers. I'm sure he must have mentioned me to you."

"He may have. We hardly ever talked on the phone. Mostly he sent me e-mails that he wrote late at night after he'd had a few beers. His life was so . . . populated, you know? I lost track of all his friends' names."

"Yeah, that was Lucky, all right. Everyone was in love with him."

I thought about how true that was.

"He never told me much about you. Were you very close?"

"We were and then . . . I don't know." I changed the subject. "Hey, where are you from, anyway?"

He chuckled. "Here and there."

"Sounds like a nice place. Is it near Oregon?"

He didn't respond. "Do you want my jacket? You're shivering."

"Nah, I'm okay."

But he took it off anyway and draped it over my shoulders. The silk lining was still warm from his body and it smelled like old leather and cloves.

He put his arm around my shoulders. Maybe it

was just to keep me warm, I don't know. We stayed like that for a minute, looking out at the water. I shifted over, even closer to him. I felt reckless. I wasn't sure what was going to happen next. He looked at me like he was deciding what to do. I tilted my chin up toward him. I wanted him to know it was okay. He leaned in like he was going to kiss me but he kissed my forehead like you would a child you were comforting. I looked away. I was embarrassed.

"Is it because of something Lucky told you about me?" I picked up a handful of sand and sifted it through my fingers.

"No. Lucky didn't tell me anything. What *about* you?"

"Nothing."

He put his hand under my chin and turned my head toward him. "Hey, I'm sorry. Tell me about you." He said softly, "Please."

"Okay." I wasn't afraid to tell him. I knew he would hear things about me soon enough anyway. Better he hear my version.

"I'm not normal," I said.

"Who is?"

"Well, I mean, I'm not dangerous or anything and I'm on meds now so I'm really okay but . . ." I paused.

"What?" He touched my shoulder. "You can tell me."

"I've done some crazy things."

"Like what?"

"Like I burned down the school."

He started to smile and then he stopped himself when he saw my grim expression. "How'd it happen?"

"You really wanna know?"

"Yes."

I swept a strand of hair behind my ear. "I was thirteen. I was having problems at school. Big problems. I'd always hated going. I couldn't focus. My teachers singled me out. They'd had Lucky in their classes and they constantly compared me to him. It made me crazy. Lucky didn't have problems like I did. Lucky didn't have problems at all, actually."

Fin leaned back in the sand and settled his weight on his elbows.

"Anyway, I was in science class. I don't remember what we were supposed to be doing, but whatever it was, I wasn't doing it. Miss Pearson, my teacher, went off on me for the thousandth time and I finally snapped. I started screaming and then I threw a globe at her. I didn't even come close to hitting her. Globes go all wonky when you throw them, but it scared her. She sent me to the principal's office but there was no way I was going there. I wandered the halls for a while and then I noticed that the door on Mr. Filipovich's storage closet was ajar."

"Who's Mr. Filipovich?"

"The school janitor. He was a total drunk."

"So I went into the closet and pulled the door shut behind me. I started poking around in his things. I was still shaking with anger. I wanted something dangerous to happen. There was a bottle of vodka way up high on a shelf, hidden behind a jar of screws. I jumped up and grabbed for it but it smashed onto the floor. I looked around for a rag to clean it up with and then I saw a pack of camels and some matches tucked behind a radio. I opened the pack and lit up a cigarette. As I tossed the match away it occurred to me that I hadn't blown it out first. The pool of vodka caught fire under my feet. Pretty much everything in that closet was flammable. I ran for the door. One can after another exploded into flames and then a whole bucket of oily rags went up. I yanked the door open and the fire reared up and tried to swallow me. It caught the back of my leg. I was so scared. I took off running down the hall and pulled the fire alarm on the way out the door." My heart pounded as I told the story. It had been years since I'd talked about the fire. I looked at Fin. He was calm.

"So, most of the school burned. Everyone made

it out. But I didn't know that. I thought I'd killed everyone. They found me curled up on the ground in the woods eight hours later."

"What were you thinking there, in the woods, I mean?"

"I wanted to die. I wanted to be ripped apart by wild animals."

He looked at me with pity. "I'm sorry."

"I'm not a bad person."

"Of course not. It was an accident. You know, I did some pretty terrible things when I was a kid too. One time I stole a car. It was just sitting there, outside a bakery, with the trunk open and the key in it, so I jumped in and I took off. I just kept driving till I ran out of gas. There was the bottom half of a wedding cake in the trunk. I ate it and then I took the subway back to Manhattan."

"Manhattan? You lived in Manhattan? Did your parents find out?"

"No. My parents died in a car accident years before that. We were living in Paris at the time. My dad was driving home from a show outside the city. He was a guitar player. My mom was in the front with him and I was asleep in the backseat. My dad fell asleep at the wheel and crashed the car. He and my mom died."

I couldn't picture anything so horrible happening to a kid. "That's awful. I'm so sorry."

"Thanks. It was a long time ago."

"Still . . ." I wanted to touch him. I thought I should comfort him, maybe take his hands in mine but something told me that's not what he wanted. We were quiet for a moment.

"So, how did you end up in New York?

"After my parents died, I was sent to live with my uncle, my dad's brother, but he lived in Bulgaria, where my parents were from before they moved to Paris. Right after I went to live with him, my uncle emigrated to New York. His plan was to open a dry cleaners in Flushing with his cousin and I went along with him."

"That must have been hard for you."

"Sure it was, at first, but it got easier."

I looked into his eyes. "Really?" He seemed to know that I wasn't just talking about him. I was talking about myself too.

"Yes. You'll see. I've had some tough times but I found a way to survive. We're tougher than you think."

"You and I?"

"Yes. You and I, we're a lot alike."

I felt a kinship with him, one I hadn't ever felt

with Lucky. "It wasn't easy, you know, growing up with someone like Lucky for a brother."

He seemed to ponder that. "It wasn't always easy being his friend, either," he said slowly.

I nodded. "But he was the best. You know, I keep thinking that he's going to come back from one of his trips? I keep thinking he'll just show up one day."

Fin sat up and put his arm around me again. I didn't know what to say. He was quiet. I felt relieved and I felt elated. Somehow Fin made me feel less lonely about my past.

"Hey, I should get you home," he said.

The last thing I wanted was to go home. I wanted a lot more of him and more of this, whatever it was, but he stood up and offered me his hand.

We made our way back up the switchbacks. In the truck he made small talk, asking me about some of the people who lived in False Bay. I chose my words carefully. I wasn't sure who I wanted to be. I wanted so much for him to like me.

He stopped at the end of my driveway. I didn't want to get out. The last hour felt like a dream. I was so attracted to him.

I tried to play it cool as I was getting out of the truck. "Thanks for the ride home," I said, smirking, before I shut the door.

"You bet." He grinned. "Remember, I still owe you that coffee."

"Right, and I'll see you at work."

After his truck disappeared down the hill, I stood outside my mom's studio a moment and watched her working on a pot. It was the first time she'd been back in her studio since Lucky died. She was bent over, completely absorbed. Eventually she sensed me watching and she looked up. She waved. I was so happy to see her working again. I wanted to tell her all about Fin but now was not the time. It would have to wait.

SEVEN

Rocket greeted me at the kitchen door and I let him outside. He needed to be walked. The sink was filled with dishes from lunch, which meant my mom ate something. I opened the fridge and closed it again. I hadn't had much of an appetite since Lucky died. I stared at the markings on a narrow strip of wall next to the fridge. My mom wrote Lucky's height with a date there in blue ink every year, from when he was two until he was fifteen and wouldn't let her measure him anymore. She didn't start measuring me till I was four. My measurements were in red ink. She stopped when I was ten.

I went to my bedroom and closed the door. I kicked my sneakers off. It was not till I was lying on my bed that I allowed myself to think about Fin. My heart began to pound. I needed to see him again. I idly picked my laptop up off the floor and turned it on. I started scrolling through the hundreds of e-mails Lucky had sent me over the last several months. Honestly, I'd never really read them that closely and then, after he died, I just couldn't. Every one of them, no matter how tired or jet-lagged or drunk Lucky was, overflowed with life. I went back to three weeks before he died and started there:

George,

Dead tired. It's midnight here and I've been out with my mates after a good long day on the water. At the bar, we got to singing Australian drinking songs with a bunch of drunken fishermen who tried to teach us the words but we couldn't understand them so we pretended. Things got ugly for a minute when their girls got a little flirty with us (can we help it if we're irresistible?). We sorted it out though and it was hugs and *I love you, man* all around. Still bunking with Javier from Spain (producer of the world's smelliest farts) and Mel from New York (trust fund recipient and bad ass surfer). My money's running low, should last about another month or so and then I have to start thinking about work. Hopefully Dad will take me on again for the summer. That won't be as bad as the chicken ranch. I almost went vegetarian over that.

Don't think I'll ever get that smell out of my nose. I'll take oysters over chickens any day. Be back home by early summer at the latest. Hug Mom for me, will you? And say hi to everyone. Miss everyone except you.

    L.

I skimmed the next several letters, looking for a mention of Fin. There were so many friends: a Javier, a Mel, a Caleb, a Donut (?), a Spark, a Jesse, and then I found him. Lucky didn't say anything specific about him, he just added him to his gang. I read back a couple of months, and then a few months before that. Fin was sprinkled all through Lucky's life, which was clear across the world, and now here he was in mine. It felt a bit strange, like I'd been given a little piece of Lucky's life as a gift.

I heard my dad coming in the back kitchen door with Rocket.

"George? You here?"

"Right here, Dad," I called out.

He opened my bedroom door. "Rocket just took a shit in the Swiss chard."

"So?"

"So, did you walk him?"

"No, did you?"

He didn't respond. I heard the back door slam

and I watched out my bedroom window as my dad took a shovel from the shed and walked over to my mom's garden. He picked up a fresh pile of dog poop and hurled it into the brush outside our property. I turned around to see Rocket staring at me from my bedroom door. He looked sheepish.

"What have you got to say for yourself?"

He turned his head to the side.

"Go get your leash, you horrible animal." I closed my laptop.

I clipped Rocket's leash on his collar and pulled on my boots. We walked past my dad, neither of us making eye contact for entirely different reasons.

"Dinner's in an hour," he called after us.

I didn't respond.

"I'm making fish stew."

I kept walking.

Rocket was a Christmas present from my parents to Lucky eight years ago. I got a bookcase that year. It was hand built by my dad. He'd painstakingly carved flowers into the wood along each side. It was beautiful but it couldn't compete with Rocket, the wiggly, cuddly, adorable puppy. I mean, what nine-year-old would choose a bookcase over a puppy? I was so despondent that I locked myself in the bathroom until hunger forced me out. When Lucky started traveling,

Rocket, who seemed to need to poop almost as often as his owner, became everyone's responsibility, and then Lucky would arrive home and Rocket was his dog again. He didn't even acknowledge any of us until Lucky took off on his next trip. But now it seemed Rocket knew that we were all he had left and he wasn't happy about it.

Rocket scampered up the back porch steps at Sonia's house. I knocked on the door. No one seemed to be around. I peered through the glass window on the door and tapped on it lightly. Sonia shuffled down the hallway from her room to the back door. She had sleep in her eyes and bedhead and she was wearing the same sweats she had on when I stopped by yesterday to try and pry her out of the house. She pulled open the door. Rocket jumped all over her.

"Hey."

"Hey, we're going down to the beach. Come with us."

She squinted into the sunlight. "Is it warm out?"

It was five p.m. and she hadn't set foot outdoors yet? This girl who used to fly down the sides of mountains most weekends?

"Warm enough . . . c'mon."

"Come inside. I'll get my jacket."

Sonia's kitchen looked a lot like ours. No food

smells though, just the smell of wood burning. Most of us here have woodstoves in our kitchens. I looked at the sink: two empty coffee cups. Sonia's mom wasn't much of a cook. She worked long hours and she had a boyfriend somewhere, Petaluma, I think, so she wasn't around that much.

Sonia pulled on a jean jacket and a wool cap. We headed downhill toward the water with Rocket tugging at the leash. We walked side by side, not saying anything for a minute.

"Hey, you remember that Fin guy from the memorial party thing?" I asked.

She hesitated. "Fin?" she said. "What about him?"

My heart started pounding again.

"Did you know he's here in False Bay?"

She stopped walking. "Really? Are you sure you mean Fin?"

"Yup. He's here. I just went to the secret beach with him."

She looked at me doubtfully and then she darkened.

"He seems really nice. You know him? I mean, from when you went to Australia?"

"Uh, yeah, I met him."

"He and Lucky were like brothers, right?"

"Uh, sure, they were friends, I guess."

"He said they were like brothers."

"Okay, like brothers."

"He picked up some shifts at the Heron."

"Waiting tables?"

"Yeah, nights."

"What the hell? I wish I'd known they were hiring. I could use a job."

"Really? You're staying?" I looked at her hopefully. "Stay, okay?"

She shrugged and looked away.

"Maybe they need more help. Jeff said the summer months are filling up. You want me to ask?"

"Nah, that's okay."

We walked across the highway and turned into the parking lot. It bothered me, her vagueness about everything. It was out of character for her. She'd always been decisive and focused. She seemed unmoored now. I don't know why it made me feel so uneasy. Maybe it was because *I* was supposed to be the hot mess in this place. Sonia always knew exactly what she wanted and then she went and got it.

The parking lot at the beach was empty except for Fin's beat-up red truck. It really was too cold for most people to be at the beach.

"That's his truck, by the way," I said.

"Fin's?"

"Yeah."

Sonia looked annoyed and shook her head. I unclipped Rocket's leash and he took off for the beach.

I fell into step with Sonia and the cold wind yanked at our hair as we stepped over the rocks and down across the packed sand to the water where Rocket was already halfway down the beach, chasing gulls. A speck of a person was walking toward us. Fin, I assumed, though he was too far away to know for sure. Rocket had spied him too and though he generally prefers seagull chasing to human interaction, he loped down the beach toward the figure. Sonia and I both watched, but we said nothing. As the figure and Rocket approached, Fin came into focus. An onlooker would probably think that Rocket belonged to him. Guys like Fin always own dogs like Rocket. Fin waved when he saw that it was us. The cold air had cleared my head and the details of my afternoon with Fin seemed less romantic now. But then he was standing in front of us and I was smiling at him and watching the way he pulled his tangled hair out of his face and how perfectly imperfect his front teeth were. He was looking at Sonia the same way he'd looked at me an hour ago. I felt a pang of jealousy.

"This must be Rocket," he said, bending over and ruffling the fur on the dog's head.

Rocket was making a ridiculous display of jumping all over him.

"Rocket! Down!" I scolded.

"Oh, don't worry. He's great. Anyway, I feel like I know him. Lucky talked about him all the time."

Lucky talked about his dog all the time but he never talked about me?

"Are you looking for waves?"

He looked down the beach. "Yeah, not much happening here today. Guess I have to drive down the coast a ways."

Sonia was hugging herself, shivering.

"Hi, Sonia," he said.

"Hi," she said softly and looked off at the water. She seemed reluctant to make eye contact.

"You look cold," he said.

"I'm fine," she said.

We stood there, awkwardly. It seemed like Fin wanted to say something to Sonia and then thought better of it. Sonia looked everywhere but at him.

"We should go," I finally said. "We need to move or we'll freeze." I didn't mean that, though. Part of me wanted to ask Fin to come with us. Part of me wanted to ask if I could go with him wherever he was headed.

"Yeah, okay. I'll see you later." He gave Rocket a quick rub. "Nice to meet ya, Buddy."

Rocket was reluctant to follow us. He stood there, watching Fin walk away. "Rocket!" I called.

When he caught up with us he circled around a couple of times, watching Fin disappear up the beach. I looked back too. Sonia didn't seem to notice.

"He's nice, isn't he?" I said, but Sonia looked lost in her own thoughts as we carried on walking.

"Sonia!"

She snapped out of it. "Sorry, what?"

"What's going on here?" I asked.

"Nothing," she said. "It's nothing."

EIGHT

"These . . . are . . . fabulous," said Jeff, with a mouth full of lavender shortbread. "You're a genius. Did Miles tell you we're going to sell them in the gift shop?"

"No." The gift shop is actually an antique bookcase next to the check-in desk.

"Well, we are, in pretty cellophane bags with a raffia tie, right next to the granola. You're not going to leave us for the big city and start a baking company, are you?"

"Why would I do that?"

"Well, don't even consider it. Miles and I had a hand in raising you. We're not about to lose you to those jaded pastry eaters in the city."

"Don't worry about it. You could pay me more, though."

Marc, who'd just strolled into the kitchen, snorted.

"Let's not get ahead of ourselves." Jeff licked his fingers. "Maybe in the summer when things pick up around here."

"It is summer."

"Almost," he said.

It was midmorning on Thursday, one of my baking days at the Inn. I generally bake Sundays or Mondays and always on Thursdays when I'm out of school and the Inn is full. Today I was making apple frangipani tarts. The pastry dough was cooling in the walk-in and I was peeling apples. The order of things, the pastry, the fruit, the assembling of desserts, it all appealed to me. I was happiest when I was working in this kitchen with all its activity and smells and sounds. I could disappear into my music or I could stay in my corner and eavesdrop on the goingson.

Marc surveyed the small mountain of apple peels. "*Tarte aux pommes?*" he asked.

"Yes, with frangipani."

"*Bon.*" He scratched his head. "I think we serve just a nice whipped cream with that, maybe almond scented, *alors?*"

"Sure, fine."

"Good morning, Marc," said Jeff, lifting the lid off a big pot of something simmering on the stove. Marc slapped his hand. Jeff retreated back over to me.

"Hey, did that new guy start yet?" I asked, casual as possible, eyes on my paring knife. I already knew that he had.

Jeff grabbed a slice of apple and popped it into his mouth. "Fin?"

"Yeah."

"He worked last night. Excellent waiter . . . and *so* attractive."

I glanced over at Marc. He never had anything good to say about the waitstaff, particularly new waitstaff. Everyone was an idiot until he decided otherwise.

"Marc, you like him?"

Marc looked up from expertly chopping shallots. He would rather I address him as "Chef Marc" and he likes to pretend that idle kitchen chitchat is beneath him, but he was quick to respond.

"He picks up the plates immediately when I set them down. Not like some of these idiots smoking outside while the food sits and sits. I could keeeees him, this Fin."

Jeff beamed. "And he's a Sagittarius. You know what that means," he said, all singsongy.

"Actually, I don't."

"Sagittarians are very compatible with Aries and Leos. And, as you know, I'm an Aries and Miles is a Leo."

Marc looked over at me and raised an eyebrow. I smiled. Jeff saw me.

"Well," he said indignantly, "when I first met Miles, I wouldn't even consider dating him until I had my astrologist's blessing."

The couple had not considered my astrological sign when they hired me. They tasted my pecan tarts at a fundraiser and hired me on the spot to "make a few desserts." Somehow, the job had morphed into full-blown pastry chef.

Jeff popped another apple slice into his mouth and glanced at his slim wristwatch. "I better go finish the wine order. I promised Fin I'd help him move in this afternoon."

"Move in?"

"He's moving into the redwood cottage. He's going to do some work on it for us and he's got some fabulous ideas for the landscaping too."

And he was gone. I stood there with a long tail of apple peel dangling from my knife, watching the swinging door, wondering if I'd heard him right. Only the most important friends of Jeff and Miles were invited to stay in the redwood cottage, and that was usually just for a weekend.

After I got the tarts into the oven and I'd cleaned up my corner of the kitchen, I wandered out to the porch and sat on the vintage porch swing flanked on both sides by distressed terra-cotta pots planted out with rosemary and oregano and placed just so by Jeff. I pushed myself back and forth on the swing with one foot. A light breeze carried the low-tide smell of rotting seaweed in from the shore.

I started thinking about last night. I'd washed and dried my hair, pulled on my favorite jeans and a T-shirt, walked down the hill, and waited for Fin outside after the dining room closed. I hadn't seen him since Sonia and I ran into him at the beach, days before. When he emerged from the back door of the Inn, I was leaning against his truck smiling. He looked surprised. He said nothing to me for a few seconds. He seemed to be considering what he should do. Then he suggested a drive. We drove in the dark, not saying much at all. Fin pulled into the parking lot above the trail we'd hiked down several days ago. I felt reckless, like I had the last time we were there. I'd never been this forward with a guy. Fin switched off the engine and watched the dark horizon. I watched Fin. This time I smelled nice. I'd prepared myself. I'd planned it carefully.

Fin inhaled abruptly and turned to me and grinned. "How about a drink."

"I'm not supposed to drink. My meds."

He frowned. "Right. Okay, well you don't mind if I do, do you?"

I shook my head. "'Course not."

"Wait right there."

He got out of the truck and I watched through the back window as he pulled a bottle of champagne out of a plastic cooler in the bed. I recognized it as the brand featured on the Inn's wine list. He got back in the truck holding the bottle.

"Ta-da!" he presented the label to me and then he pulled off the foil and the wire cage like an expert and tossed it on the floor. I wondered if he'd intended to share it with someone else.

"Miles will kill you if he notices. He does rigorous inventory, you know."

"Don't worry, I'll replace it tomorrow. He won't even know it's gone."

I smiled.

"Hey, wanna see a cool trick?"

"Sure."

He leaned over me, so close that I could smell his hair. He popped open the glove box and pulled out a bone-handled hunting knife. He extended the blade carefully.

"This won't hurt a bit." He pulled a knob on his dash. His high beams came on, eerily lighting the fog swirling up from below the cliff. He jumped out of the truck.

"Watch." He stood in front of the truck like a magician on a stage with the bottle in one hand and the knife in the other. He held the champagne by the bottom and with his other hand he ran the knife quickly up the side of the bottle. There was a loud pop and the entire top of the bottle and the cork shot off into the darkness. Champagne foamed up over the freshly cut glass rim. I squealed and clapped my hands. He bowed dramatically and got back in the truck.

"That was so cool!"

"Here, hold this," he handed me the bottle and pulled a thermos out from under the seat. He unscrewed the metal cup. I looked at the bottle. The top was sliced off cleanly as though he'd used a glass cutter. He took the bottle from me and filled the cup. He handed it to me. "Madame?"

I hesitated, and then took a small sip. It was ice cold and delicious. Warmth spread through my belly.

"Where did you learn that?" I asked.

"My dad."

I handed him the cup and he took a thirsty swig. He refilled it. I couldn't take my eyes off him.

"I'm not as interesting as you think I am" he said, like he was reading my mind.

"Are you kidding? Paris, New York, Bulgaria?"

"It wasn't like you think. A lot of my life has been hard times. After my uncle and I moved to New York he got deported back to Bulgaria and I should have been too but there was no way I was going. My family left Bulgaria for Paris when I was three. I couldn't even speak the language. I couldn't go back there. After my uncle left I took off. I became a street kid for a while. I even spent some time in Crossroads."

"What's Crossroads?"

"It's a place for juvenile delinquents in New York. I got caught stealing stuff, just small stuff: electronics, CDs, things I could sell so I could eat. They put me in a foster home but I took off again. I lived like an animal."

"That sounds terrible," I said. I pictured him darting furtively around the streets of New York City, staying one step ahead of the law.

He offered me the cup again and I shook my head. "Better not."

"How long have you been on your meds?"

"Forever, seems like." I stared out the windshield. "They make me feel like I'm not here," I said, turning to face him. "Do you know that I haven't even cried since Lucky died? Not one single tear."

"It's okay," he said. He wrapped his arms around

me and pulled me to him. He felt warm and strong and I didn't want him to let me go. He pulled away first.

Fin dropped me at home. I kissed him on the cheek and he said he would call me soon. I lay awake all night thinking about him: the way he looked at me, the way he smelled, the way he knew how I felt. When I finally fell asleep I dreamt of Lucky, but this dream was different from the others. In this dream something was pulling him down through the dark water, away from me. I tried to swim after him but I was pathetically slow. I woke up exhausted. All day at work I'd been replaying my night with Fin.

I was about to go back to the kitchen to check on my tarts when I heard a car approaching from the other direction and turned my head out of small-town habit to see who was coming up the road. I recognized Fin's red truck and my heart leapt. He turned into the lane just before the Inn. Jeff and Miles live on that lane. His window was rolled down and I could see that he was having an animated conversation with his passenger. He was so preoccupied that he didn't even glance over at the Inn or the porch where I was sitting in plain view. Then I recognized the person in the passenger seat. It was Sonia. She was listening to something Fin was saying and though she was far away, I thought she looked upset. I wondered how they came to be driving down the road together. Had she climbed right in beside him just like I had? I pulled my cell phone out of my apron and dialed her cell number. Her voice came on the line: *Hi, you've reached Sonia. Leave a message and I'll call you back.*

I clicked my phone off.

NINE

I rode shotgun in Sonia's mom's car as we made our way along the winding Coast Highway to a café in Bodega. Sonia called earlier and asked me to come along with her. The band playing at the café were Lucky's friends. I'd met them weeks ago at the party, though I hardly remembered. Sonia told me I'd like the music and that it was time we got out and did something. She was right. The open wound of Lucky's death had started to heal around the edges and I was glad to get out. I also wanted to know what she was doing in Fin's truck on Thursday. I wanted to know if he'd touched her like he'd touched me. And had he pulled away from her too or was she the reason I got taken home early? I looked over at Sonia as she navigated a curve in the road. Some of the color had come back into her face and she seemed almost excited to be going somewhere on a Saturday night. She'd even managed to throw together some clean clothes that showed off her figure; nothing special: a long-sleeved black sweater and jeans, but for weeks now she'd been wearing clothes that said *I don't care.* I smelled perfume on her too. That was new. I never knew her to wear perfume. Maybe it was her mom's. I desperately wanted to question her but I also wanted her to *want* to tell me what had happened. I mean, why wouldn't she?

"So, I called you Thursday but you didn't pick up. I saw you in Fin's truck, though."

Sonia looked over at me. Her eyes narrowed a bit like she was trying to figure out what I already knew. "We drove down to Jenner."

"Yeah? What did you do there?"

She looked back at the road. "Not much, had a glass of wine. Then we went for a walk on Goat Rock Beach."

"Guy likes to walk on the beach a lot, doesn't he?"

She didn't say anything for a few seconds and then she turned to me.

"It's not like you're thinking. I needed to talk to him."

"About what?"

"About Lucky."

"You can talk to *me* about Lucky."

She let out an exasperated sigh. "I know," she said, and then she seemed to remember that I'd lost Lucky too. "I know I can. I'm sorry. You've been great."

We drove along in silence for a minute.

When I thought about Fin with Sonia, I was envious. Were my trips to the beach with Fin about getting to Sonia? I'd made it very clear that I was interested in him, but not much had happened. Why had he been so tender with me? And what about the champagne trick? Wasn't that just for me? Plus, he'd shared so much about himself with me. I'd thought about little else but him since that night.

The day before, there had been an e-mail in my inbox from another friend of Lucky's, a guy named Jesse, back in Australia. I remembered Lucky mentioning him. In the e-mail, Jesse said that he and Lucky had been "the best of mates" even though Lucky hadn't been in "Oz" long. He said he couldn't afford to fly out for the party but that they had their own Aussie-style memorial on the beach for Lucky with a bonfire and lots of singing and playing Lucky's favorite songs. He wanted to tell me and my mom and dad how sorry he was and that Lucky was a hell of a nice guy. He said Lucky could "carve" like no other surfer out there and that was a tough thing for an Aussie to admit, being that Lucky was American. He also said that it still "boggles the mind" that Lucky, of all the surfers he knew, could die like that. There was no one who knew water better than Lucky, he said. I wrote back and thanked him. And though I'm not sure why, I asked him if he knew a friend of Lucky's named Fin. I already knew the answer to that question but I couldn't resist finding out more about him.

Sonia slowed the car down and steered it inland toward Bodega and now we were driving along redwood-lined roads. The light was quickly disappearing behind us. The fields on either side of the road turned to forest and the approaching twilight swallowed us up. Sonya slid her sunglasses onto the top of her head. It was a rare fogless evening. Normally by this hour, an inky-gray mist would be unfurling itself like a fist slowly opening, creeping further and further inland, but not tonight.

I looked up at the sky through the windshield and broke the silence. "There's going to be a billion stars out tonight."

Sonia looked up too. "At least a billion." She smiled at me. She wanted us to be okay. I did too.

The dirt parking lot was jammed with cars. This area is rife with musicians and music people and tiny clubs and cafés. I'd never been to this club before but

Sonia told me that she came here lots of times with Lucky. It was one of their favorite spots.

We sat down at one of the last open tables, to the left of the stage. The people sitting at other tables were your usual mix of year-round, off-the-grid, coastal dwellers; pretty girls who looked high, wearing no makeup and out-of-date dresses from India, the kind you buy in stores that smell of incense. The men were ruddy cheeked with messy beards and the children had dirty faces and looked too young to be up this late. We ordered from a hippie girl in a ruffled peasant blouse and a long skirt. I was dying to get a real drink but I ordered iced tea. I didn't want to risk her asking for ID and embarrassing me. Sonia ordered a beer.

"It's nice here, isn't it?" she said, looking around. She waved at someone she knew across the room.

"Uh-huh." I felt a rush of anxiety like I always do when I'm in a crowded room. I took some deep breaths, in through my nose, out through my mouth. Dr. Saul taught me this. I soon felt calmer and I smiled at Sonia, who was watching me with concern.

"Okay?"

"Yup."

The musicians, two guitarists and a stand-up bass player, stepped onto the stage. The audience clapped and whooped the way they do when the person onstage is their neighbor or their brother-in-law or their plumber or Bruce Springsteen. The band started in on a warm-up, a brisk little gypsy jazz guitar tune. They were very good. One guitarist played lead and the other played rhythm, but then the rhythm player took a lead and showed off a bit. He nodded when the crowd clapped. At the end of the song, after the applause died down, the lead guitarist, a serious-looking guy with small glasses and feminine features, spoke into a microphone.

"Thanks very much. That was 'Minor Swing' by Django Reinhardt. We're The Hot Club of the Lost Coast and we'll do our very best to entertain you with some tunes tonight. We've got a special treat for you now. A new friend of ours is going to join us up here for a set. Please help us welcome him. Come on up here, Fin."

Sonia and I looked at each other. She seemed as surprised as I was. Fin approached the stage from the back of the café. I hadn't seen him back there. How was it possible that he'd already endeared himself to these people? He looked quite different from the Fin I'd met several days ago. He was wearing a porkpie hat, a black vest, and a crisp white shirt with the sleeves rolled up. It was more of a costume than an outfit. He sat in a chair next to the rhythm player and picked up a small weathered guitar from a stand next to him. There was an expectant air in the room. He was the new kid and everyone, including me, wanted to see if he had the guitar chops to keep up with this crowd.

Fin said nothing to the audience, but he nodded his head to the other musicians and counted them in. When they started to play I immediately recognized the tune from one of my mother's many Django Reinhardt CDs, the ones she puts on when she wants to gaze out her studio window moodily and smoke. Fin's long fingers flew deftly up and down the fretboard. The other two guitarists were smiling as they tried to keep up. Fin kept time by tapping his pointy black boot on the wooden stage. He made it look so easy, like he was born to play. Sonia laughed and looked at me. She leaned closer. "Can you believe this?" she whispered in my ear.

"Did you know he was coming?" I asked her.

She shook her head. "No, I swear."

I looked around the room. The energy had shifted and intensified. Everyone was leaning forward in their seats. All eyes were on Fin, even the little kids were mesmerized. I was pulled in with the rest them. Where had he learned to play like this? Then I remembered that he'd said his dad played guitar. But hadn't he also said that his dad died when Fin was still a kid?

Fin looked like an angel up there on the stage, a beautiful, mysterious, smooth skinned, dark-eyed angel. I watched Sonia's face. I could almost feel her falling for him. How could she not? Fin looked up and he nudged the other players into solos and took over the rhythm. His eyes traveled around the room and landed on me. I felt myself blushing. I looked down at my iced tea. Then he looked at Sonia. She didn't smile but there was something there, like they shared a secret.

The song ended and the crowd let loose with applause and cheering. Fin nodded and smiled like someone who's used to playing for crowds, someone who knows he's good.

On the way home, driving through the darkness, I thought about how those people reacted to Fin's playing. When the set was over, Fin moved through the room, ruffling a toddler's hair, shaking hands, thanking people. As we were on our way out, Fin took Sonia's arm. I waited by the door. They had their heads together, talking. Sonia shook her head but Fin kept talking and eventually she nodded. I knew that they must be planning to meet up later. I felt cast aside. He caught my eye as I was leaving and smiled but I gave him my stoniest expression. How did he *think* I would feel?

Sonia was preoccupied as she drove through the darkness.

"Did you tell Fin where you were going tonight?" I asked.

She looked at me. "I'm not sure. I guess I may have."

"I wonder why he wouldn't tell you he was playing with those guys."

"I dunno. Maybe he wanted to surprise us."

"You. Maybe he wanted to surprise *you*."

She looked over at me. "Okay."

"You seem totally into him."

"Do I?" She looked flustered. "It's just the music, I think. It got to me."

"Did you know he could play like that?"

She paused. I'd started noticing that whenever she answered a question about Fin, she seemed to choose her words very carefully.

"I guess I knew he could play, not like that, though."

I sat back in my seat and looked at my reflection in the window. Sure, lots of surfers play guitar. But players like I saw tonight are the kind of people who practice for hours a day and study under virtuosos. Players like that think of little else but their playing. And why didn't he play at Lucky's party, I wondered.

Sonia dropped me at my house. I felt very much like the little sister, sent home so the big kids could play. I had feelings for Fin that I probably shouldn't have, but so what? Maybe he was just a welcome distraction from the gloom that had descended on me since Lucky died. Maybe I was hungry for that kind of attention. It felt nice for a minute.

I poked my head into the living room. My mom was curled up on the sofa reading a book. She looked up at me and smiled. My dad dozed in front of the TV. Rocket lifted his head for a second and went immediately back to sleep on the braided rug. Even though everything looked perfectly normal, something about that scene made me feel unbearably sad. There was a hole in my family I could never fix by myself.

I went to my room and checked my e-mail before I pulled off my clothes. There was a message from Jesse. I clicked it open even though I felt a bit guilty, poking around like this. But I couldn't get the image of Fin up there onstage out of my head.

Georgia,

Of course I remember Fin. He was part of our merry throng. Hell of a nice bloke. You could ask Sonia about him if you're in touch with her. I think she and Lucky and Fin might have taken a road trip down to Sydney to do some surfing there together. I reckon she could tell you all about it if you asked her.

Cheers, Jesse

I stared at my computer screen. So . . . Sonia, Lucky, and Fin had gone on a road trip together? Why hadn't Sonia mentioned it to me? And hadn't Sonia told me that they barely knew each other?

I opened up my laptop and started sifting through all of Lucky's e-mails again, dragging all the letters that contained an attachment into a folder. The only attachments he ever sent were photos. Once I'd divided them up I started clicking on them, one at a time. Fin's face started popping up a couple of months after Lucky had arrived in Australia. In the photos he didn't look much like the Fin from tonight at all. He fit right in with the rest of the surfers. There were lots of photos of him standing on a beach with a bunch of Lucky's surfer friends. I stopped on one of those and zoomed in. Fin looked disheveled. His chin was sprinkled with beard stubble and his hair was pulled into a hasty ponytail. I zoomed back out. It must have been the end of the day. Everyone had their wetsuits peeled down to their waists and they looked sunburned and spent and each of them held a can of beer. This was the sort of thing I envied most about Lucky, this talent for making friends. Fin stood on the far left of the group while Lucky was on the far right. Everyone was grinning at the camera except Fin. Fin was grinning at Lucky.

TEN

The next morning, walking down the hill to the highway, I was thinking about Fin and Sonia. I was still wondering why Sonia had lied to me about how well they knew each other. Something strange was going on.

A damp mist in the air was falling invisibly onto my hair. I shivered and pulled the hood of my gray sweatshirt up over my head and started up the highway toward Katy's.

Common sense told me I shouldn't ask Sonia about any of this yet. I knew there was a good chance I'd end up feeling hurt again, but when I got to Katy's I impulsively called her.

"Did you sleep with him?" I surprised myself

by blurting out a question that I knew was none of my business. I hated the way I sounded like a jealous girlfriend.

"No," said Sonia. "And, by the way, it's not really any of your business."

It was childish of me to even ask but I needed to know. I pictured her rolling her eyes and wanting to get off the phone.

"Is he there?" Another dumb question. I'd just walked past her house.

"No. Of course not." She sighed. I was humiliating myself.

I tried to rationalize everything that was happening: Lucky was Sonia's first boyfriend. Lucky is dead. Fin knew Lucky. Sonia knows Fin. If I thought about it like that, it made perfect sense. And could I really blame Sonia? I saw Fin last night too, up on the stage. I'd have done the same thing if he'd asked me instead of her. I'd have gone home with him.

But then there was the matter of Fin just showing up in False Bay . . . and staying. Was I the only one who thought that was a little weird?

"I'm sorry," I said.

"Look, it wasn't like you're thinking. That music was so . . . I don't know, but it got me talking about

Lucky. So, that's what we did. We talked about Lucky. I've just felt so numb till now. But last night I cried. It felt good to cry. Fin cried too."

I dropped the phone by my side for a few seconds and squeezed my eyes shut, imagining that. I hadn't cried yet. Was I numb like Sonia? Or was it the meds? Several times I'd punched the wall with my fist until my fingers felt broken and I was exhausted. Then I passed out, and then I had the nightmares.

I heard Sonia's voice and brought the phone back to my ear. "I'm here."

I watched out the window as Sharona's beat-up Toyota wagon pulled off the highway into Katy's tiny parking lot. I glanced at my watch. She was forty-seven minutes late. Not that it mattered. It was gloomy outside, not the kind of morning where kites and taffy spring to mind. I'd had three customers. Even though we were officially on the summer schedule, one person could handle Sundays like these. I touched my hand against the side of Sharona's latte. It was lukewarm.

"I'll call you later," I told Sonia.

"Sure. But don't be mad. It's crazy to be mad."

"I'm not mad," I said. And I wasn't. I guess I was just jealous.

I clicked the phone off. Sharona's car door swung open, and she threw a cigarette butt onto the ground and stepped on it. She exhaled a plume of smoke into the wind and yanked her handbag out of the car, throwing it over her shoulder. The bell on the door jangled.

"Sorry, sorry, sorry." She breezed in, dropping her handbag next to the cash register. "I would have called but my freakin' cell phone died right after I got a flat on the Coast Highway. This mine?" She grabbed her latte and gulped it. "Mmmmm."

"You want me to put it in the microwave?"

"Nah. So, I'm on the side of the highway, pulling the spare out of my trunk, though God knows what I intended to do after that, and that guy, what's his name again? Fish?"

"You mean Fin?"

"Yeah, that guy is *so* nice. Is he seeing anyone?"

I shrugged.

"Anyway, he pulled over and just like that, he changed my tire for me. It was like he was my guardian angel. I get a flat and boom! He's right there. I coulda kissed him. I think I did, actually."

Was there anyone around here who hadn't been dazzled by Fin yet?

Sharona stepped into the tiny bathroom and left the door open. "Look at me. I'm a mess." She rearranged her hair and applied lipstick. "Did Katy call yet?"

"She did. I covered for you. I told her you ran out to get change."

"You're awesome."

"Hey, was there anyone with Fin when you saw him?"

"No, just his dog. A sweet black-and-white mutt. He looked a lot like your dog, actually." She blotted her red lipstick on a tissue and tossed it into the trash.

Wait, Fin doesn't have a dog. That *was* my dog, I mean Lucky's dog. What was Fin doing with Rocket in his truck?

Sharona started chattering away like she always does. She liked to catch me up on the highlights of her Saturday night, which was always eventful. The cast of characters in Sharona's life was colorful and her circle of "friends" seemed to extend far out in every direction. I only half listened to her. I was still preoccupied with Fin and how every time I turned around, he had dug himself just a little bit deeper into my brother's old life.

Was I being paranoid? I winced as I thought about something that happened a couple of years ago. I had noticed that a drifter I'd seen around town looked just like a guy wanted for murder in North Dakota whose picture I saw on a poster hanging in the post office. Apparently, I'm the only person in town who actually reads those. I tried to convince everyone I spoke to that we had to turn him in. By then the drifter had been hired by Ralph at the gas station. The guy turned out not to be *that* guy, and I had to avoid the gas station till he left town a year later.

I dug a bottle of aspirin out of my backpack, popped the top off, and shook one out.

"You got a headache again?"

"Yeah." I swallowed it with the last bit of my luke-warm coffee. The headaches always started at the base of my neck and crawled up my scalp to the backs of my eyes. That's when I couldn't stand it anymore and I had to take an aspirin or two.

"Hey, Sharona, would you mind closing alone to-day? I've got a lot of baking to do at the Inn now that they're selling the cookies in the 'gift shop.'" I used finger quotes.

"Sure, no problem. I owe you big time."

"Thanks." I massaged the back of my neck, lost in thought.

ELEVEN

I pulled the back delivery door of the Inn open just in time to hear Marc hurling half French, half English insults at someone. I made my way tentatively to the kitchen. Marc was waving a stainless-steel spoon at the oily grime that Karl had left on the stovetop. I guess he couldn't even get near it without a weapon. Apparently, Karl had left the kitchen in less-than-premium condition after the brunch shift. I'm sure he got slammed this morning. For the first time this season, all twelve of the Inn rooms were occupied for the weekend.

Jeff and Miles were running interference.

"If you could just keep your voice down, I'm sure we can get this place cleaned up in no time," said Jeff.

"We? Oh, no, no, no, I don't clean up after that *connard*!"

Miles cracked the swinging door an inch to check on the dining room. Over his shoulder I saw a few couples lingering with their afternoon coffee. They were looking in the direction of the kitchen with puzzled expressions. Miles let the door close softly and made alarmed eye contact with Jeff.

I snuck quietly over to the prep table and started working while Jeff and Miles tried to calm the red-faced Marc. I watched and waited for an opportunity to slip out and check on something I'd been musing over all day. The first batch of cookie dough only took me a few minutes. I quickly rolled it into four logs and wrapped them in plastic wrap. I put them in the walk-in to chill and then I slipped out of the kitchen unnoticed. The door to Miles's ex–broom closet office was open and I was relieved to see that his computer was turned on. I clicked the mouse and it came awake. The payroll file was right on the desktop. I clicked on it. I could still hear Marc yelling. He was threatening to quit, calling them amateurs. The file opened. I scanned the list of employees, searching for Fin's name. It wasn't there. I went through the list again. The only name that wasn't familiar to me was Abel Sacula. I was confused. Was it Fin's real name? I jotted it down on a piece of paper and shoved it in my pocket. I also happened to glance at what they were paying Marc as opposed to Karl. For what that prima donna was making, a little cleanup from time to time wouldn't kill him.

I could still hear raised voices in the kitchen, so I quickly googled the name Abel Sacula. I tapped my finger impatiently. Nothing came up for Abel Sacula, but a few links appeared for the surname with connections to Bulgaria. I quickly read a link. Someone calling themselves Violeta Violina had posted on a message board: *I am looking for members of my family from Bulgaria with the surname Sacula, my maiden name. I know that my great-grandfather was Romani with family near Sofia and I am interested in learning more about my Romani heritage . . .*

Romani? I googled the word and clicked on a link. I scanned the article: *"The Romani people are also known by a variety of other names such as Gypsies and Roma."* Fin did look exotic and he certainly had gypsy jazz in his blood. Had Fin's dad been Romani? I was intrigued. Why wasn't that part of the story he told me?

I clicked the computer back to sleep. Miles would kill me if he found me in here. I peeked into the kitchen where things seemed to have simmered down for now. Jeff was wiping down the cooktop himself while Marc chopped up vegetables and dropped them into a stockpot, still grumbling in French. Miles was pouring a generous glass of the Heron's best French red. He placed it in front of Marc: a peace offering. Marc still had his pouty face on but he picked up the glass and took a big gulp. He wiped his mouth on the back of his hand. Then Fin appeared next to him, seemingly out of nowhere. Marc smiled and greeted him in French. Fin responded in perfect French. Of course he spoke French.

"Tout ce spectacle, c'était juste pour le vin?"

Marc laughed and clapped Fin on the shoulder. *"Eh bien, il est assez bon, ce vin. Je prends un autre verre?"*

Fin shook his head. *"Je ne pousserais pas si j'étais vous. Ces deux là sont très pingre avec le vin."*

"Pas qu'avec le vin, ils sont radins comme tout," said Marc, and they laughed together like old friends—like old *French* friends. Miles and Jeff watched the exchange with amusement, even though it seemed that Fin and Marc were talking about them.

I stood there watching through a crack in the door for a couple of minutes. Fin's accent was beautiful. I could have stood there listening all day.

Fin seemed to be leaving. I guess he wasn't on the schedule for dinner service. *"Adieu. À bientôt,"* he said to Marc. To Jeff and Miles he said, "Later, gentlemen."

They both grinned. "Bye, Fin," they said in unison. They were head over heels in love.

After I finished baking the cookies and pulled two trays of plum and cardamom crisps in individual ramekins from the oven, I set everything to cool on the prep table and I hung up my apron. The kitchen was peaceful for a moment but the staff would arrive soon to start setting up for dinner service. I left out the back door and walked briskly home up the hill. The sky looked ominous. It was still early evening, but the fog had never really pulled back all day. I was tired and my headache had returned. I really wanted to talk to Sonia, but I doubted she wanted to talk to me after this morning's conversation. I was starting to feel something strangely unsettling about Fin, but I decided to keep it to myself for now. Fin was just what this town sorely needed: a good dose of charm and a fresh face. Who was I to get in the way of that?

As I neared my house, I saw Fin's red truck parked in the driveway. My pulse quickened. My first thought was that he'd come to see me. The house was dark, though. My dad wasn't home yet, but my mom's studio glowed warmly through the tall windows. I stood off to the side, hidden by the creeping jasmine, and watched through the studio window. Fin was sprawled in my mom's old wicker chair, holding a large handmade mug in his lap. He rubbed Rocket's belly with his bare foot. Rocket was passed out next to him on the wooden floor. My mom was perched on a stool a few feet away, burnishing a pot on the canvas-covered worktable. She vigorously rubbed a small polished piece of glass against the outside of the large pot, bringing the surface to a soft sheen. Her forearm looked strong and sinewy, and a strand of hair fell across her eye. She looked a bit like Georgia O'Keeffe, my namesake. I couldn't hear what they were saying, but I could see their lips moving. My mom didn't look up when she spoke. She seemed very comfortable having Fin sit there, watching her.

I'd never sat in that chair long myself. My mom had always shooed me away after a few moments, claiming that I was distracting her. I was a fidgety kid. I could never sit still. Watching Fin, so comfortable in that chair, and so comfortable in his own skin as he watched my mom, I felt envious again. I also felt protective of my mom and her space. But she was smiling slightly. She looked focused and calm. She seemed not to mind that Fin had crossed boundaries I wouldn't cross, boundaries that had been in place since I was a little kid. She laughed at something Fin said and looked over at him coyly. It was clear now who he came to see. He was here to charm my mother the same way he'd been charming every living thing in his path, including me, since he arrived.

I let myself into the darkened house through the

kitchen door and flicked on some lights. There was a damp chill in the air. I started a fire with kindling in the woodstove and added a few logs once it got going. My laptop was on the kitchen table. I quickly typed in Abel Sacula again. This time an article from a French newspaper appeared. The headline read: *"Guitariste célèbre tué dans un accident de voiture."* I tried to read the article but could only figure out a word here and there. It seemed to say something about a car accident. In the middle, there was a grainy black-and-white photo of a man who looked an awful lot like Fin playing guitar. Underneath the photo it said, *"Yuri Sacula, sur scène."* I worked my way through the article, word by word, as though my French might improve if I kept at it long enough, but it just frustrated me.

I got up and put a kettle on for tea. Then I sat down again and clicked through some more links till I found one in English. It was a story in a British guitar magazine about Yuri Sacula, a famous gypsy jazz guitarist from Bulgaria. This had to be Fin's dad. There was a better photo here too. Yuri was attractive in the same way that Fin was. He had the same dark expressive eyes and the same bemused smile. The article said that Yuri was married to a woman named Sophie. There had been a car accident outside Paris and Yuri and Sophie were killed. The gypsy jazz guitar world mourned the loss of a magnificent player, it said. It mentioned that the couple's son Abel had survived the accident, but there was nothing about what happened to him after that. Fin's story checked out. He was who he said he was. Why wasn't I more pleased about that?

I got up and looked out the window at the studio. The two of them were still there. The kettle whistled and I shut the burner off. I browsed the fridge. Dad had left a colander full of clams on a plate. I'm sure he had plans for them, but I needed to do something, so I started working on linguine and clam sauce: I gathered up parsley, garlic, white wine, olive oil, lemon. We had no shallots but onions would do. As I was chopping the garlic, I heard the kitchen door open. My mom was laughing. It was possible that this was the first time I'd heard her laugh since before Lucky died. Suddenly she and Fin were standing together in front of me. My mom's cheeks were pink and her eyes were dancing the way they used to when she and Lucky would go on their walks on the beach and they would come back full of ideas. Rocket gave me a halfhearted greeting and returned to Fin's side.

"I didn't see you come home, Honey." My mom kissed my cheek.

"I thought I'd better get a fire going. It was so chilly in here." I kept chopping.

"Have you met Fin, Lucky's friend? Oh, I forgot, of course you have."

She said "Lucky's friend" like it was all the endorsement she needed, like it was the passcode to gain him access to everything that was Lucky's.

"Uh-huh." I looked up. "Hi." My heart pounded in my chest. I felt a twinge of guilt, like I'd been reading his diary. The story of how he was orphaned was terribly sad, but he seemed so self-assured that it was hard to think of him as the little boy who'd lost both his parents in one moment.

He grinned at me. "Hi, George." He seemed to need to explain to me what he was doing here. "I was just returning Rocket. We went on a field trip together, didn't we, Boy?"

Rocket, hearing his name, did a quick happy circle around Fin and then looked at me just in case I may not be aware that this Fin guy really knew how to show a dog a good time. It occurred to me that Rocket must have been in Fin's truck when he stopped off at the Inn a couple of hours ago.

"Looks like you've made a friend," I said, finally looking him straight in the eye. "Looks like you've made lots of friends."

He was still smiling with not even a hint of

sheepishness in his eyes. He looked at the clock over the table. "It's getting late. I should get going," he said.

"Really? Can't you stay for dinner? We've got lots," said my mom. She touched the sleeve of his pale blue linen shirt. Her eyes sparkled. "He should stay, shouldn't he, George?"

"Absolutely," I said. Almost all of me *did* want him to stay even though I intentionally sounded sarcastic. I would not let him know how conflicted I was feeling, but I wanted desperately to touch him. I wanted to be near him.

He watched me. "Another time," he said.

My mom looked disappointed. "Okay, then. Another time. Promise?"

"I promise."

"Oh, wait, let me grab that book I was telling you about." She went into the living room, leaving me alone with Fin.

He plucked a stem of parsley off the cutting board and put it in his mouth. "Your mom is incredible. I see now where you get it."

"Thank you," I said. "Hey, by the way, I looked up your dad online. He wasn't just some guitar player. He was really famous." I watched Fin for a reaction.

He didn't respond at all. It was almost like he

hadn't heard me. I rubbed the back of my neck. My headache was back with a vengeance.

I tried again. "And Jesse says hi."

He looked at me with a deeper intensity in his eyes. "You're really suffering with those headaches, aren't you? You should get off your meds. The sooner, the better. They're poison."

"Found it!" called my mom from the other room. She returned with the book *The Philosophy of Andy Warhol*. She handed it to him. "Take your time with it. You'll see what I mean about him."

"Thank you, Madeleine." He kissed her cheek.

"Bye, George." He waited for me to acknowledge it.

I tried to look nonchalant. "Bye."

"Hey, maybe you could come along next time."

"Next time?"

"Next time I come for Rocket."

This is a regular thing now, you in my house?

Rocket jumped up on him and gave him a slobbery kiss, sensing that this was good-bye. "Till then, Rocket Man!" he said.

As he turned to leave he looked back at me. "And say hi to Jesse for me, okay? I owe that guy a letter." He didn't wait for my reaction. He was already out the door.

My mom opened the fridge and pulled out the colander of clams. She looked at the ingredients on the chopping board.

"Linguine and clams? That sounds good. I'll put on the water for the pasta." She hummed to herself while she ran the water into the big pot at the sink. I dropped a tea bag into a mug and grabbed the kettle off the stove with a potholder.

"Tea?" I asked my mom.

"No. I'm drowning in it. Thanks."

I poured boiled water into the mug.

"Fin's awfully nice, don't you think?" she said.

"I suppose."

She caught something in my voice. She looked over at me from the sink.

"Have you been taking your meds?"

"Yes, of course I've been taking my meds. Why?"

"Nothing. You just look a bit pale, that's all."

"I'm fine. I just have a headache. And yes, I took some aspirin."

"Okay. Anyway, I think he's very nice."

"But you don't really know him, do you?"

She paused a moment, thinking. "You know, I guess I don't know him at all but I feel like I've known him for years. Isn't that strange? Has that ever happened to you?"

I shook my head. I wasn't sure I wanted this conversation to go any further.

"It's like he exudes this consoling vibe." She shook her head. "Maybe I'm just imagining it because he was close to Lucky. Maybe that's it."

"Could be. Is there lettuce? I was thinking about making a salad." I went to the fridge to check. My mom seemed not to have heard me. She was gazing into the pot she just filled with water and smiling slightly like she was remembering something pleasant. I stood behind her and squeezed her shoulder. She patted my hand absentmindedly. I looked out the window, squinting past our reflection in the glass.

Fin's truck was still in the driveway with the motor running. His shadowy figure was sitting in the dark, watching us. He seemed to know that I'd seen him because he quickly put the truck in gear and backed out of the driveway.

TWELVE

Dr. Saul watched me impassively from his cracked leather chair.

"I'm getting more headaches," I said. "It's the meds."

He stroked his beard and blinked behind his little silver-rimmed glasses. This was not the first time I'd complained about the meds. We'd tried several different ones: Clozaril, Geodon, Risperidone, and now Seroquel. We'd also tried combinations: a bit of this, a bit of that, but the meds were always problematic. There were side effects: lethargy, dry mouth, depression, suicidal thoughts, weight gain, weight loss, nausea, appetite loss, and headaches. I'd experienced all of them.

"I was reading about Famotidine online. It looks promising," I said.

"It's still in trials for schizophrenia. It won't be approved for years."

"So, now what?"

"I'll adjust the dosage again," he said.

I sighed heavily. I was so tired of this adjusting, changing, adding in, taking out. "I don't want to adjust the dosage. I want off them. Can't we just try? Just to see what happens. I've been fine for ages. Maybe I *am* fine. Maybe I'm better. Hey, Doc, maybe you've healed me."

"It doesn't work like that, George. We've talked about this. I hope I don't have to tell you again. I'm sorry."

I looked out the window at the alpacas cantering around the paddock. Dr. Saul's wife, Peggy, raises them for the wool, which she spins herself on an old wood spinning wheel and sells from a little workshop on the other side of the property.

Dr. Saul is an unconventional psychiatrist. He and Peggy are Deadheads. They met at a Grateful Dead concert back when they were young hippies and they spent years following the band all over America in a VW microbus. Dr. Saul's office is an old log cabin. Any wall space that isn't taken up with bookshelves features Dead posters from all the shows he and Peggy have been to. Also, colorful drums from their weekly drum circle are stacked up next to the fieldstone fireplace. The room smells of wood smoke and incense.

I started seeing Dr. Saul right after the fire. Back then he took scribbled notes when we spoke. My mom came along with me at first. Dr. Saul asked me what kind of a kid I remembered being and I blurted out, "Gifted, creative, maybe a bit emotional. "Then he had a private conference with my mom and I'm sure she filled in all the blanks about me: Prone to hysteria and fits; suspicious, paranoid, and possessive; a loner, quiet, withdrawn, and moody but capable of flying into an unprovoked rage. I really hoped she didn't use the word "dangerous" because I wasn't, even though I'd heard it whispered behind my back.

School was very difficult for me; some days it was impossible. I couldn't seem to make friends and there had been incidents, lots of them. Dr. Saul took me off Ritalin, which Dr. Garcia, our family doctor, had put me on years ago. Once I was off the drugs I felt better for a time, but then I began to notice some changes in myself. I felt like there was a committee in my brain. They took every thought I had and fed it through a device that twisted it or fouled it up or misconstrued it and then fed it back to me. I wasn't in control of my own thoughts anymore. I started coming unglued. I was sure that I was being followed. I read secret messages meant only for me in road signs and billboards. I was convinced that some of my classmates wanted to kill me. I believed I had killed people with my thoughts.

Right after I turned sixteen, Dr. Saul sent me to San Francisco for some tests at a clinic in the University of California. They were very nice to me there. They gave me a CT scan so they could look at my brain and an EEG so they could chart my brain waves. They asked me hundreds of questions about myself and they did blood and urine tests and they took some spinal fluid, which was horribly painful. They asked my mom about our family, her parents and my dad's parents, aunts, uncles, everybody. My mom took me to Chinatown for Chinese food when we were done. I remember having a nice time with her that day. I still have the fortune from my fortune cookie in my jewelry box: *You will soon uncover a happy secret,* it said.

When he got the results of all the tests, Dr. Saul told me that I was most likely suffering from chronic paranoid schizophrenia. He told me that I didn't need to worry, that there were good drugs and we would keep it under control. He said that I could live a normal life, or almost normal. That's when he started me on meds. I am nowhere near normal.

Dr. Saul's golden retriever, Jerry, asleep at Dr.

Saul's feet, made a whimpering sound and flicked his paws like he was dreaming about running. Out the window I could see Jerry's sister Janis in the paddock, annoying the alpacas.

"My brother died and all I cared about was getting my lemon tarts right for the party," I said, still looking out the window.

"That's perfectly normal. It's a coping mechanism."

"And I haven't cried yet." I looked at him.

He blinked and said nothing.

"I'm sick of it. I'm sick of feeling shitty or feeling nothing."

"I understand, Georgia."

"I haven't had an incident in a really long time. How will I ever know if I'm okay if I never get off the meds?"

"Georgia, you know better than that. The drug has built up in your system. If you stop taking it, the results could be disastrous, and then you'd have to start all over again."

"That's okay. I don't mind. I promise I'll start again if it doesn't work. Can't we just try?" I looked at him pleadingly.

"I'll lower your dosage. It might help with the headaches, but I want to see you in two weeks for an assessment and I want you to call me immediately if you notice any changes. I know that these sessions are private, but I want you to let your mom know what we're doing, okay? She needs to know to keep an eye on you."

"Deal."

"And this is a trial only."

"I know, I know, I know." I smiled.

Dr. Saul scratched a prescription onto a pad.

This was the best I could do. I knew I could never persuade Dr. Saul to take me off my meds completely. But if I could cut back a bit at a time, and he could see an improvement, maybe eventually I could get him to let me stop taking them completely. I just wanted a chance to see who I could be without them. Maybe I could be normal. Maybe I could be happy. Maybe someone like Fin could love me.

THIRTEEN

The next morning I took my first pill of the day with a sip of water. It was the first day in a long time that I would take two pills a day instead of three. I wanted it to feel like the start of something new for me. I wanted to feel hopeful. I brushed my teeth and looked at my face in the bathroom mirror from all angles. My expression was pensive. Pensive was my default face unless I consciously arranged my features otherwise and stayed completely focused. I would have to try to remember to smile more. Why was smiling so hard for me? I produced a wide confident smile and started a conversation with the mirror. "Hi! My name's Georgia," I said. "Great to meet you. Fine, thanks. How are you?" I tried to look like the carefree, fun-loving girl in the deodorant commercial on TV. I turned around and looked back over my shoulder at the mirror. I swung an imaginary tennis racket and bashed my knuckles on the glass shower door. "Damnit!" I squeezed the pain away with my other hand. I looked in the mirror again. I was back to pensive.

After breakfast I went to my bedroom and sat cross-legged on the rug next to my bed. I closed my eyes and tried to clear my mind. I took a deep cleansing breath in through my nose and out through my mouth. I repeated this ten times. I opened one eye. Rocket was panting warm dog-food-scented breath onto my bare leg. He wanted to go for a walk. What he really wanted was Fin, but Fin hadn't been around for several days and I was a very distant second choice for a beach-walking companion.

I looked at Rocket's eager face. "Sure. I bet he can throw a stick pretty far but does he know where the dog treats are kept? Does he?"

Damnit. I was thinking about Fin again. That was not supposed to happen today. I abandoned the cleansing breaths and grabbed my laptop off the floor. I checked my e-mail as though I were someone who got e-mails. No new mail. Lucky was really the only person who ever e-mailed me. Rocket stood up and barked once.

"Okay, okay. Let's go." Rocket ran for the back

door. I clipped his leash on and let him drag me out the door and down the hill toward Sonia's house. I hadn't talked to her since our awkward phone call. There was a spiral of woodsmoke curling out of her chimney and her mom's car was gone. I stopped along the way and picked a bunch of blackberries that had just come ripe, the first of the season. I pulled a plastic bag out of my pocket, meant for Rocket's poop, and filled it with berries. Rocket watched me with interest. I knocked on Sonia's back door and when she opened it I held up the bag of berries.

"Look."

She smiled. Her hair, which was honey blond the last time I saw her and all her life, was now the color of the berries in the bag. I'd never known her to dye her hair before.

"Wow. Your hair."

She touched her hair. "Yeah, it's a bit dark but it'll fade."

"To what?" I couldn't imagine.

"I needed a change. I just didn't feel like being me anymore."

"Mission accomplished. Come for a walk?"

Sonia held the door open for us, and Rocket tore off down the hallway. He sniffed the place out while I went into the kitchen and got a bowl out of the cupboard and dumped the berries into it. My hands were stained to match Sonia's hair almost exactly. I rinsed them in the sink and watched the deep purple swirl down the drain. Sonia disappeared into her bedroom and reappeared with her hair piled on top of her head. Besides her face, which was now quite pale in contrast to the hair, something else about her looked very different. Her eyebrows. They'd been tweezed into an alluring arch, like a movie star's. Plus, she was wearing lipstick. It was a deep-plum color. I studied her a moment as she pulled on her jean jacket and wrapped a bright-green scarf around her neck. She looked a bit tragic, but very pretty, like a French woman, like she should light up a cigarette and exhale in that exquisite way that actresses in French films do. I was certain that Fin had something to do with the new Sonia. Had he actually coaxed her into changing the way she looked?

Sonia knew I was scrutinizing her but she said nothing. "Shall we?" she looked at me.

"*Oui!*" I called for Rocket and he bounded ahead of us out the door.

Afterward, we walked over to the Heron for a coffee. We left Rocket passed out on the porch. Not once on our walk had either of us mentioned Fin, the elephant in every room. I was dying to ask her about him, but I forced myself to wait for her to bring him up in conversation. The restaurant was empty except for an older, well-dressed couple in the corner, enjoying a late breakfast. The sun beamed in through the tall windows onto the rustic wooden floor.

"So I guess you heard that Fin's got a full-time gig with The Hot Club."

I hadn't heard.

"Wow. That sounds kind of permanent."

"Yeah, I guess."

"Are you happy?" *Are you having sex with him? What's that like? What's it like to be naked with him? What's it like to spend the night with him?* That's what I really wanted to know.

She looked away uncomfortably. "I suppose."

I wondered when I would get up the nerve to ask her what she knew about Fin that she wasn't telling me. Obviously he wasn't just a friend of Lucky's who was holding her hand through this. Now that some time had passed, I realized that it had to have been Fin who had chased her out onto the porch at the party that night. Hadn't she said *You shouldn't have come*? What was that all about? It was true. She'd still be wearing stained sweatpants and sleeping all afternoon if Fin hadn't arrived with his extraordinary talent and his devilish charm and his extreme sense of goodwill.

But there was something more to this. Something had happened in Australia between the three of them.

"Where's he from, I wonder?" I tried to sound like I was just musing. Sonia waved at someone. I turned around. Karl had emerged from the kitchen, his breakfast shift over. He yanked the beer cooler open and put a Heineken down on the bar. He waved at me and grabbed a handful of spiced cashews from a bowl.

"I don't know. Oregon, I think." Sonia sipped her coffee.

"Really?" *I think?* How could she not know?

"Yeah, why?" she asked.

"No reason, just curious."

Sonia looked at me like she wanted to say something.

"What?" I said.

"Nothing. It's just that . . . oh, forget it."

"No, tell me. Please."

"It's just that I don't want my relationship with Fin to upset you. You seem a little revved up about it. I hope you understand how important you are to me. You're my family. I love you. I would never let some guy come between us. I've told Fin that. He totally understands . . . and I get how you feel. I really do. I mean, he's not Lucky, but you do know that he's not trying to be . . . right?"

"Of course," I said, but with very little conviction. I looked out the window at the restaurant garden. *I'm* revved up? If Fin were just "some guy" she wouldn't have purple hair right now. I felt silly though. She thought I was looking out for Lucky, even though he's dead. And, in a way, I guess I was. But I was also looking out for myself. I wished more than anything that Lucky had told me about Fin and what had happened between them on that road trip to Sydney. And now he couldn't.

Suddenly Sonia's eyes lit up and fixed on something over my shoulder. She smiled the smile I'd been trying for in the mirror that morning. And then Fin was standing next to our table.

"Two pretty girls. Lucky me," he said. He leaned over and kissed Sonia on the lips. Her eyes flickered my way and then back to him. Fin straightened and he rested his hand on my shoulder. "Hi, George."

"Hi."

He squeezed my shoulder hard. "What are you girls whispering about?"

I looked away. He dropped his hand.

"Sit," said Sonia. "Join us."

"I can't. I'm driving up to Petaluma with Miles to pick up a smoker he bought. I'd better go find him. I have to be back for my shift at four-thirty."

"Okay," she said.

"I'll see you later," he said. "Bye, George."

I smiled thinly.

Fin nodded hello to Karl, who was wiping down the bar, and then he disappeared through the swinging door into the kitchen.

FOURTEEN

Lucky stood in the foreground, waving at the camera. His friends looked on from behind him, laughing.

"Hey, everyone! Here I am Down Under. As you can see." He gestured behind him. "I've fallen in with a disreputable bunch of scallywags, clearly not worthy of my company, but I took pity on them, poor disparate souls that they are." The video was all shaky and the audio was pretty garbled.

Jesse turned the camera around to his own face, which appeared comically huge.

"Cocky, isn't he? And did he say 'Down Under'? I reckon we ought to take the bugger down a notch or two." He turned the camera on a group of guys who piled onto Lucky, knocking him down into the sand.

"That's it, lads," yelled Jesse from behind the camera. "Show that Yank some Aussie love!"

My eyes welled up.

Jesse kept yelling and laughing from behind the camera.

The video had arrived by e-mail early this morning with this note:

George,

Came across this terrible video I took of all of us. I know it's not much, we were just mucking about, but I thought you might like to have it. I recorded it a couple of hours before Lucky died. Apologies for the quality and for all the swearing. Cheers, J.

I paused the video on the pile-up of Lucky's pals in the sand. I quickly located Fin in that pile. It was so strange to see his familiar face right next to my brother's. I clicked "play" again.

"Get off me, you drongos," yelled Lucky.

I got back into bed with my laptop. I pulled the covers up over my head, making a tent, and watched the video over and over. It was only a few minutes long and it ended with all of them grabbing their boards and heading into the water. I couldn't stop watching that part where Lucky spoke to the camera. Having him here and alive and safe in my bed with me made me hang on every precious word. How many times had I told him to shut up? Now I wished he would just keep talking. Every time I pressed "play" again I hoped he would say a bit more. I wanted just a few more minutes with him. Then the tears finally came, rolling down my cheeks, soaking my pillow. I heard Rocket's toenails clicking across the wooden floor. I pulled the sheet back and he pushed his face into my tent. He cocked his head to the side when he heard Lucky's voice. I played the video again and he barked and wagged his tail. He smudged my laptop screen with his wet nose and then he tried to lap up my tears.

"I know, right, boy?" I patted his head.

Since Dr. Saul had reduced my dosage, my headaches were fading. The vice-grip on my skull had been replaced by a pressure against the back of my head, sort of like a hand pressing down, but not so hard that I couldn't bear it. The world seemed to be coming into a sharper focus. The edges of things had returned. I loved the way I was starting to feel, like I was slowly unthawing after being numb for years. I wanted to feel a lot more like that. Not being drugged was like a drug. I was waking up. It didn't matter that it hurt sometimes, the way it hurt to watch the video. I embraced it. And I wanted more of it.

Late the night before, while the house was quiet, I had pulled a steak knife from the cutlery drawer in the kitchen and taken it into my room. I closed the door and sat at my desk. I meticulously sawed several of the little white pills in half, being very careful not to crumble them. Dr. Saul told me never to cut the pills. I didn't care. I put the tiny half-moons back into an empty prescription bottle and hid it inside a pair of socks in my sock drawer. As of this morning, I was down to one and half pills a day. It wasn't like I was going cold turkey. I would reduce the dosage slowly, gently. My body wanted this. A new me was emerging.

I wondered if I should show Jesse's video to my mom, but lately she'd been doing so well, I didn't want to ruin it. Ever since the night Fin dropped by it seemed that everything about her had lightened: her mood, her clothes, she even seemed lighter on her feet. The deep lines of pain on her face had started to soften and she'd found her smile again. She was wearing her colorful scarves and necklaces too. She hummed while she worked and she was eating again. Our family routine, which revolved around my mom's work, was falling back into place. I couldn't help but think that

Fin had something to do with it. To my mom, Fin was probably a lot better place of refuge than Lucky's clothes or his bed. After all, Fin was a friend, a "good" friend of Lucky's, but something about all of it seemed wrong to me.

I decided not to show her the video.

I was late for work. Katy would be calling. The store should have been open ten minutes ago. I finally closed my laptop and got out of bed, but I wanted to watch that video all day.

I got myself to the store and spent the day loathing my job. Fortunately, the store required little of me in the way of interacting with the customers. The candy speaks for itself. It's over there. Help yourself.

I dialed the new, improved Sonia's number. I wanted to tell her about the video. I thought she might want to see it. She picked up after several rings. She sounded sleepy.

"Hi George."

"Did I wake you?"

"Nah, I have to get up. What's up?"

"You know Jesse, Lucky's friend in Australia?"

"Sure."

"He sent me a video."

She was quiet a few seconds. "Yeah? What kind of video?"

"Of Lucky and some friends, on the beach. Fin's in it too."

"Yeah?" she seemed nervous.

"Hang on."

A customer, a very large flushed woman wearing flowered capri pants and a hoodie from the Monterey Bay Aquarium stood in front of me.

"Can I help you?" I asked, holding my hand over the phone.

"Yes. Do you have the nutritional information for the taffy?"

"Uh, nutritional information?"

"Yes, you should have it available to customers. It's the law."

"I'm sorry. I don't. No one's ever asked me for it before."

"It's the law."

"Yeah. You said that. I can call my boss if you like."

She looked annoyed. "It should be posted. Some people have food allergies."

"Would you like a kite instead?" I offered.

I uncovered the phone. "Hey, I've gotta go. I'll send you the video, okay?"

"Sure. Okay."

The woman drifted off toward the taffy bins and started filling up a bag.

FIFTEEN

"Hey, Georgie." My dad grinned at me from the driver's side window of his truck. "Hop in." He was wearing a wool beanie and polarized sunglasses.

I crossed in front of the truck and jumped in next to him. The cab smelled like the ocean when the ocean smells bad. I kissed his stubbly cheek.

"You looked lost in thought," he said, as he steered the truck up the long hill to our house.

I shrugged "Nah. Just trying to remember if I set the alarm at Katy's."

"You want me to swing past?"

"No. I'm pretty sure I did. What's new at the farm?'

He sighed heavily. "Busy busy. Can't complain about the business but it's a lot of work this time of year . . . tourist season. Most restaurants are doubling their orders. I guess I got used to your brother turning up every year around this time to help out. You know, I used to think that he would show up when he ran out of money, but now I realize that he showed up right when I needed him most." He was quiet for a few seconds, like he was considering that. "Yeah, I'll probably hire someone. I should have thought of that but I just . . . I don't know."

I did that too. I kept expecting Lucky to show up at the breakfast table. My dad expected him to pull up in his beater at the oyster farm.

When we got to the house, Fin's truck was parked in our driveway again. My pulse quickened. My dad was oblivious. Here in False Bay, unexpected visitors are a matter of course.

"Looks like we've got company," he said. He pulled up beside Fin's truck and I jumped out and peered into the cab.

"What are you doing?" he asked.

"Nothing."

There was a tennis ball on the seat, Rocket's, and a bright green scarf, Sonia's.

"I think I smell lasagna," my dad said, pulling open the back door.

We heard my mom's laughter coming from the kitchen. She was in the middle of telling Fin a story about a trip our family took to Mexico when Lucky was nine and I was five.

"... and then we finally locate our nine-year-old kid and he's pulling himself up the side of this sheer cliff with a bunch of these crazy Mexicans who've been drinking tequila on the beach all afternoon. I started shrieking like a madwoman, running down the beach, waving my arms, and the little bugger, he waves at me and he yells something like, *Hi, Mom, watch me jump,* though I can't hear him. So off the cliff he goes, arms flapping like a baby bird. I almost had a heart attack. Theo and I trip over ourselves to get to the water, ready to dive in, and his little blond head pops up like a cork and he swims to shore like an Olympian." She laughed again and then she stopped abruptly and took a sip of her wine. She looked over her shoulder at us. "Hi, guys. Look who stopped by."

My dad shook hands with Fin. I said hi, though I wanted to say, *Why? Why do you keep showing up like this?* It was pretty obvious he wasn't here to see me. He smiled that smile I'd become all too familiar with.

A vase of freshly picked wildflowers sat in the middle of the table with a bottle of red wine next to it. My mom took another sip from her glass. There was another glass of wine in front of Fin, who was sitting in Lucky's chair at the table. No one had sat in that chair since Lucky died. Fin was wearing a brown sweater. The cuffs were stretched out and it looked soft and worn. It was the kind of sweater that you're compelled to touch even when a stranger is wearing it, even if it's someone standing in front of you in line at the grocery store. It was all I could do not to reach out. Fin's hair was tucked behind his ears, making him look especially earnest. In spite of everything, I wanted him to wrap his arms around me and kiss me right that second.

"Hey, I made lasagna," said my mom. "Fin's staying." Her cheeks were flushed from the wine.

Fin looked up at me again with a wide grin that seemed to say *I'm in.*

"I'll check on that lasagna." I retreated to the oven.

Over dinner, I started to understand how he did it: how he skillfully deflected any questions that might connect him to a place, a family, or a home, or a past. He responded with *here and there* and *around* and *this and that.* He asked a lot more questions than he answered and he seemed keen to know about other people's lives, which was disarming and charming at the same time.

"I hear you're playing with the Hot Club," said my dad. "Those guys are pretty good. Where'd you learn to play guitar like that?"

"Oh, uh, Julliard," said Fin, as though he were

saying *community college*. *Julliard?* He went to *Julliard?* How in the hell did he go from being a street kid to Julliard?

"Fin, that's a wonderful school. I'm very impressed!" said my mom.

Fin shrugged and refilled my mom's wineglass.

I wanted to file that piece of vital information for later, but at the moment it was clanging around my head like a pair of garbage can lids.

"I used to play a little myself but I'm not sure I can keep up with a Julliard graduate," said my dad.

"Course you can. I'll bring my guitar over next time."

"I'll have to dust mine off. I'm not even sure where I put that thing. The strings are probably dead."

"I'll restring it for you if you like," said Fin.

Things were getting pretty cozy. I changed the subject. "Is Fin your real name?"

Fin took a sip of his wine and shot me a bit of a dark look. "It's a nickname. You know, because I'm in the water a lot."

But he *wasn't* in the water a lot. As far as I could tell, he hadn't been surfing once since he'd arrived.

Fin started a conversation with my mom about her art. Then he asked my dad about oyster farming. More wine was poured and soon the room was filled with laughter and my parents were treating their new friend like he was their long-lost son. My jaw started to clench. My dad started pulling out all his favorite jazz CDs and putting them on. He was getting excited, remembering concerts and clubs he went to "back in the day." Fin was right there with him. He knew music even better than Lucky had. I gathered up the empty plates and carried them to the kitchen. As I set them down on the counter, it occurred to me again that Fin had slipped right into Lucky's life like it was a vacant parking space. He hadn't counted on resistance from Lucky's little sister, though. I sat down again at the table and Fin's knee brushed against my thigh. I kept my leg there, with his knee pressing into my thigh. I stared at him, daring him to move it. He held my gaze. It seemed like he was physically trying to coax me onboard with everyone else who was falling for him.

I excused myself and went to the bathroom. Then I slipped into my bedroom and opened my laptop and looked around till I found a site for Julliard alumni. I typed in "Abel Sacula" and clicked "search." Suddenly he was there on my screen, staring out at me with those dark eyes. His hair was a lot shorter, but he was the same guy who was sitting at my table with my parents right now. The contact part of his bio was blank. Everything else seemed to match up, though. The dates made sense.

He was a Julliard graduate all right. Laughter and music drifted in from the other room. Then it got quiet. I looked up. The knob on my bedroom door turned slowly and the door opened. Fin's face appeared.

"Oh, sorry. I thought this was the bathroom." He looked at my laptop and I resisted the urge to slam it shut.

"It's the next door down."

"Okay. You coming back? Your mom's got pie."

"I'll be right there. Just checking my e-mail."

His eyes lingered on mine for a few seconds and then he slowly closed the door.

I listened for the bathroom door to close but I heard nothing. I tiptoed across the floor and turned the doorknob quietly and opened the door an inch, peering out. The bathroom was empty. The door stood wide open. Then I heard footsteps on wood. Fin was in Lucky's room. I carefully closed my door and waited. I heard a drawer slowly slide open and then closed. Several minutes later I heard him walk back up the hallway. Had he taken something of Lucky's?

When I finally got back to the table, they'd polished off a second bottle of wine. My mom was in the kitchen, slicing up homemade blackberry pie. I watched as my dad offered Fin Lucky's job at the oyster farm. I felt powerless at what was happening under everyone's noses. Something snapped in my brain. I had to say something.

"Really, Dad," I said. "Lucky's job? Isn't it bad enough that he's sitting in Lucky's chair, eating dinner with Lucky's parents with Lucky's dog at his feet? Next thing you know he'll be sleeping in Lucky's bed. Can't you see what's happening here?"

The room went silent. All three of them stared at me with varying degrees of shock. My mom held a plate with a slice of pie on it in midair.

Fin's lips curled slowly into a smile. "Wow, George, did you take your meds today?"

My mom looked at Fin and then back at me. "Honey, he didn't mean anything by sitting there, and your dad needs someone at the farm. I think you should apologize to Fin."

My dad looked confused.

I was humiliated. My face went hot. Fin darkened when I looked at him again. The smile had vanished. He seemed to be telling me to stop this . . . or else. A flutter of fear ran through me. I stood up and pushed my chair back. I left the room.

I heard my mom apologizing for me and explaining that I'd had a tough time lately. Fin responded graciously. No one seemed to see what had just happened. Not the way I saw it, anyway.

SIXTEEN

My mother started policing my meds as instructed by Dr. Saul, who put me back on my old dosage. Three times a day she poured me a glass of water, shook a pill out of the bottle, handed it to me, and watched me swallow. She soon stopped asking me to open my mouth and stick out my tongue and lift it up so she could peer under it. She made a big deal about "trusting me." She never saw me slide the pill between the inside of my cheek and my molars. The bitterness made me fight the urge to gag. As soon as she was out of sight I spit the pill into my hand and threw it out my bedroom window. Then I brushed my teeth vigorously.

My mom kept me close now. Things that she used to do alone she now did with me. I know that she valued her alone time and she probably resented having me along.

"Do you wish it was me?" I asked as we drove north along the coast.

"Do I wish it was you what?"

"Instead of Lucky, do you wish it was me?"

She took her eyes off the road to look at me. "No, of course not. Don't say things like that."

"It's okay if you do. I wish it was me too."

She looked exasperated. "Please, Georgia. Stop."

My mom was gearing up to do a wood firing. She used to teach pottery classes and her eager students would fall all over themselves to help, but now she's too busy with her own work and gallery shows to teach, so she's making me help her. Years ago, my dad built the stone kiln in the backyard. It sits in the middle of a sandpit. It's hot and dangerous. The fire needs to be stoked every few hours and it has to stay blazing hot. Earlier that morning, we stacked a cord of wood that the wood guy delivered. Then we got in the car. Seaweed is a big component of these wood firings. My mom adds it along with some other organic things like rice and tea leaves to the kiln to give each pot a unique finish. The best seaweed is down toward Fort Ross, right near where we scattered Lucky's ashes. My mom parked the car in the dirt lot and we trudged down the rocky beach in rubber boots.

"Gross!" I said, as I picked up the disgusting-smelling seaweed and dropped it into a big garbage bag. "Really gross, Mom!"

"It's not that bad," she said.

The sun was out but it was cold and windy and the beach was deserted except for a flock of gulls that sat hunkered down in the sand, watching us with mild interest.

Thousands of tiny flies swarmed over the piles. I kicked at each pile to scatter them before I could touch the seaweed with my gloved hand, but they still flew up into my face. I was chilled and miserable. With a full bag each, my mom and I started trudging through the wet sand, dragging our heavy bags across the beach to the car. Something compelled me to turn around and look back out at the choppy water. I shielded my eyes from the sun and looked for the spot where we'd scattered Lucky's ashes. A head popped up out of the water, a seal of course, it had to be a seal, but then I saw blond curls and an arm waving for help.

"George! Help me!" I heard Lucky calling out to me.

I dropped my bag and start running back toward the water. My boots were heavy and slow in the sand but I kept my eye on the bobbing head and the waving arm.

"Lucky!" I called out to him, running in slow motion. "Lucky, I'm coming!"

My mom caught up to me and tackled me from behind just as a wave retreated and I was finally getting some traction on the wet sand. We hit the ground and rolled around.

"Let go of me!" I shrieked. I couldn't believe she was trying to pin me. I squirmed around, trying to get out from under her, straining to see above the wave that was fast approaching. I had to get to Lucky.

"Mom, it's Lucky. We have to help him. Get the hell off me!"

My mom got up and pulled me roughly to my feet. "Look!" She pointed. "It's a seal."

I looked out at a glossy black-headed seal, bobbing in a wave, watching the commotion on the shore with curiosity. I scanned the horizon for that blond head. It was gone. I had to wait for him to resurface.

"I heard him, Mom! He was calling me."

"Seagulls," she said. She wrapped her strong arms around me and pulled me firmly to her. "Stop it, baby. You're scaring me." She said this quietly into my ear. I looked up at her, my eyes filled with tears. "I saw him, Mom. I did."

She held my face in her rough hands and kissed my cheek. She dropped her hands to her sides and stalked over to her bag of seaweed. I stood watching the water, waiting.

"Georgia, let's go!" called my mom. I finally followed her and we trudged side by side up the beach, dragging the bags across the sand. I looked over my shoulder again and again, all the way up the beach.

SEVENTEEN

From my bedroom window I watched my mom in her studio. She was examining the pots she'd pulled from her kiln the day before, picking up one at a time and slowly turning them to see every side. She put one down in the center of her worktable and picked up her camera and took a photo of it.

A few days had passed since the incident at the beach so my mom wasn't watching me quite as closely anymore. I'd been planning a trip down to Fin's cottage for a while and now seemed like a good time to slip away unnoticed. I wasn't entirely sure what I was looking for but I would know when I saw it. I pulled on my jeans and left out the back door. I started down the hill, walking briskly. I knew that Fin was out of his place because I'd listened from my room when he picked up Rocket earlier.

When I got close to Jeff and Miles's house, I slowed my pace and tried to look casual, like I was out for a stroll. I turned into their drive. It was all clear. I looked around and quickly crossed the lawn to the cottage at the back of the property. The redwood on the exterior was weather-worn to a smooth silver. Red-and-white-checkered curtains hung in the window. It looked like a fairy-tale place.

The latch on the wooden door gave easily. Once inside, I walked around the small cabin, making sure that there were no signs that anyone was there. I looked out the window. All was quiet except for the gentle rolling sound of the waves and the crows cawing in the redwoods. An Italian coffeemaker sat on the small stove. The side of it felt barely warm. There were two used coffee mugs on the countertop, one with Sonia's bright lipstick on the edge. A plastic honey bear sat next to the mugs. Honey dripped down its belly. All around me were mementos of a couple in love: rocks and shells picked up on the beach and carefully lined up on a wooden shelf, candles burned down to nubs, a half-full bottle of red wine with the cork forced back in, and the white sheets on the unmade bed entwined like the ghosts of lovers. On the top of the dresser in a driftwood frame there was a photo of Lucky, Fin, and Sonia. I picked it up. It was taken on a beach in Australia. Sonia is in the middle and has her arms around both guys' waists.

Fin's guitar leaned against a straight-backed wooden chair. I went to it and picked it up carefully. The finish was worn down to the bare wood where a pick had rubbed against it thousands of times. On the back of the neck, the initials *YS* were burned into the wood in curly script—Yuri Sacula, Fin's dad. I set it down. I pulled open the wooden drawers on an old carved dresser. Most of them contained piles of Fin's neatly folded clothing: T-shirts, sweaters, a couple of pairs of jeans. I tried the bottom drawer but it was locked. The lock was old. I looked around for a key but Fin probably had it with him and I'd never picked a lock in my life so that wasn't an option. I sat down on the floor and braced my feet against the feet of the dresser and gave the drawer a really good yank. The lock broke and the drawer flew open, pitching me backward. Jeff and Miles would die if they saw me do that.

The drawer was empty except for a handmade wooden box. I took it out and opened it. Inside there was a stack of photos, an old necklace, a few guitar picks, and a simple silver signet ring engraved with the initials *YS* again. I leaned against the bed and looked carefully at the first picture. It was a black-and-white photo of a darkly handsome man wearing a white shirt with the sleeves rolled up. It was Yuri Sacula. He was sitting in a wooden chair holding a small, dark-haired Fin on his lap. Fin was grinning at the camera. The resemblance to his dad was uncanny. Behind them on the table were the remains of a meal: a breadboard with a knife, the end of a baguette, a chunk of cheese, and an empty bottle of wine with glasses at two places. The background looked like a bohemian apartment. The photographer must have been Fin's mom, Sophie. In the next photo, Yuri sat on a stage, playing guitar. He was wearing a finely tailored dark suit. A cigarette dangled from his mouth and his face looked just like Fin's did at the club that night, like there was nothing in the world but the music. I looked closely at his hands. He was wearing the signet ring. A stand-up bass player and a rhythm guitar player were onstage with him, also in suits. In the third photo Fin and his dad were sitting across from each other, playing guitar. Fin looked about six years old. He was leaning over his small guitar, intently studying his dad's fingers. Then there was a photo of a very attractive woman in a stylish dress and heels. This had to be Sophie. She was walking up a narrow cobblestone street, carrying a straw bag in one hand. Her other hand held Fin's little hand. Her deep-red hair was swept up into an updo and she wore bold red lipstick. Almost every detail matched exactly the way Sonia looked now. She was smiling alluringly at the photographer. Fin was looking up at his mother with great affection. He had on a little pair of trousers and a tweed newsboy cap. He looked about four years old.

The next one was taken on a boat somewhere. A boy, about eighteen, was standing at the railing. He was tan and windblown. He looked like the privileged son of wealthy parents. I wondered how he fit into Fin's life. The last group of photos were candid, it seemed. They were pictures of Lucky and Sonia. In one they were walking along a beach, talking, looking solemn. There were a few of Sonia asleep in the backseat of a car and one of Lucky and Sonia asleep together in a bed—Lucky's arm was slung over Sonia's waist from behind. There was one of Lucky showering at the beach. And then several of Sonia walking, laughing, swimming, reading a book, surfing. Then there were a few of the boy from the boat photo: a couple of him asleep in bed, possibly taken the same night. Had Fin watched him sleep? A few others of the boy were taken through the window of a café where he's sipping coffee and looking lost in thought, or perhaps he was waiting for someone. It was clear to me that these photos weren't meant to be seen by anyone but Fin. I exhaled. I'd been holding my breath. The photos proved nothing but they offered me a glimpse of a dark side of Fin I'd started to suspect.

As I put the photos back I noticed a note folded up at the bottom of the box. I removed it and unfolded it quickly. My hands were shaking now. The note was written in French with a fountain pen. I refolded it and stuffed it into the pocket of my jeans.

I tried lamely to fix the lock but it was no use. The next time Fin opened this drawer he would know that someone had been in here.

I sat on the bed and looked around. I felt desperately alone. I kept finding myself in places that my rational mind had nothing to do with. The things that I was putting together about Fin were just too sensational to fit into my safe sleepy life here in False Bay. I was scared. I wanted more than anything to go back to the way things used to be but it was too late. Something kept pushing me on, or maybe it was *someone*. Maybe it was Lucky.

EIGHTEEN

I walked home, uneasy about what I'd just done. I sat at the kitchen table, lost in thought, but then I took my laptop into Lucky's room. Rocket was still on a date with Fin. My mom was still out in her studio and my dad was at the farm. The house was quiet. There were bits of Rocket's fur on the quilt in the shape of a curled-up dog. No one bothered to shoo him off the bed anymore.

I sat down on the bed and typed "Yuri Sacula" into my browser again. Links to shows all over the world where Yuri had performed popped up. I clicked on them, one by one, and watched. Some of them were higher-quality videos from concert halls in Europe and some of them were grainy videos shot in smoky, crowded clubs. Everything about the way Fin moved, the way he smiled, the way he played guitar, it was all just like his dad. Between songs, Yuri would speak to the audience in French. He always had a lit cigarette dangling from his mouth.

Holy shit. Fin was only ten when his parents died.

I pulled the note I'd taken from the wooden box out of my pocket. It was written in a very feminine hand. The heavy linen paper was creased and looked like it had been read over and over. I laid it next to me on the bed and typed it carefully, word by word, into a French/English translation site. When I was done, I clicked "translate" and read the note:

My sweet little sausage, I am sorry I wasn't there to pick you up from school today. Your father and I had to take the train to Lyon this afternoon. He is playing a concert and then we will catch the train home late tonight. I will kiss you while you sleep and you will see me in the morning when you open your eyes. Be a good boy for Kiki and she will give you a nice piece of honey cake for your dessert. Sweet dreams. I love you very much. Mommy.

I should never have taken the note. It obviously meant a lot to him. I had to get it back into that box somehow. I folded it up and tucked it into my pocket.

I curled up on my side, thinking about Abel and

the life he'd already lived by the time he was ten years old. And the life he'd lived after that. What had it all led him to? What had he become? A charismatic adventurer who moved around a lot, charming people everywhere he went? Or was he a coldhearted seducer who was hiding something awful? The idea that the latter could be true had been bubbling around in my brain for some time now, but I finally let it move to the forefront of my thoughts. Had Fin murdered my brother so he could have his life?

I thought about the day my brother died as I gazed up at a famous surfer on a poster taped to the wall above Lucky's bed. A wall of water as big as a building was coming up behind him. The spray from the top of the wave was raining down on him. My eyes became heavy.

I guess I must have drifted off. When I woke up it was dark in the house. I sat up and called out "Mom? Dad?" I heard nothing. I put my feet down on the floor. Water rushed over them. There was water on the floor, at least an inch deep. It flowed in from the door. I jumped up and splashed through it in my bare feet. The house was empty. Where was everybody?

I ran outside. On the road in front of my house a black car had crashed into a big oak tree. It looked like the car had knocked over a fire hydrant before it smashed into the tree. The front of the car was crumpled up against the tree and a fountain of water was shooting straight up from the hydrant. The car was old. It was the kind you see in black-and-white gangster movies. On the passenger's side, a beautiful redheaded woman rested her head against the window. A tiny trickle of blood ran down her forehead. She looked like she was sleeping peacefully. There was a snowflake of shattered glass on the driver's side with blood in the center. The back door of the car slowly creaked open and a frightened dark-haired boy peered out.

"Little boy!" I called out to him. He looked at me and took off running. I ran after him.

"Little boy, please stop!"

A river of water gushed down the hill next to him as he ran. "Please stop. I want to help you!"

He kept running. My bare feet were scraped and raw from the pavement. He reached the bottom of the hill and turned right on the dark, deserted highway. There was no one around. I was starting to fall behind.

Finally, I called out, "Abel!" He stopped short and turned to look at me. He looked confused at how I knew his name.

I closed in on him. He darted off the highway

and ducked into the underbrush on the side of the road. I followed. I could hear him rustling in the dense growth. I got closer. I could almost touch him.

"Please! I'm not going to hurt you!" I reached out for the sleeve of his blue shirt and held on. He turned around and spat "*Lâchez-moi!*" He yanked his arm away and quickly fought his way through the tangled undergrowth until he was in a clearing. He kept running. I watched him until he disappeared.

"George," I heard my dad's voice. "George, come eat."

I slowly opened my eyes. I was still on Lucky's bed. I rolled over and looked at the floor. It was completely dry. I got up and walked down the hallway and out the back door. My dad watched me from the kitchen, puzzled. I followed the walkway out to the street. There was no car, no water. There wasn't even a fire hydrant. What was happening to me?

I heard Fin's truck rumbling up the hill as I stood there in the middle of the road. He pulled up next to me and rolled down his window. I couldn't look at him the same way anymore. I felt ashamed. My fingers touched the note in my pocket.

"You okay? You look a bit dazed."

Rocket was in the passenger seat.

"I'm fine."

"So, uh, I was just at my place and it looks like someone broke in. You wouldn't happen to know anything about that, would you?" He held my eyes with a look that made a chill run up the back of my neck.

I shook my head. "Can I have my dog?"

"Lucky's dog? Sure." He leaned over and opened the passenger door. Rocket jumped to the ground and ran up the path to the house.

"Careful, George," he said.

I watched him watching me in his rearview mirror as he drove away slowly.

NINETEEN

I called Dr. Saul's voice mail and canceled my appointment. With every pill I didn't take I felt stronger and I felt more awake. The headaches had stopped completely and tiny rushes of clarity fluttered through me like electric currents. I had the sudden urge to ride my bike. I found it out in the garage behind a rusted barbeque and some folding lawn chairs. It was covered in a thick layer of dust and both tires were flat. I couldn't remember the last time I'd ridden it. Lucky's bike looked as though someone had ridden it yesterday. I decided to take his instead.

I coasted down the hill to the post office to pick up our mail. There was a slip inside our PO box, a notification of a package. I went inside and handed it to Myrna, our postmistress and the town busybody.

"Hang on a tic, dear. Lemme grab that for you," she said.

She came back with a shoebox-sized package. "Here you are. Looks like it's all the way from Australia." Myrna always reads return addresses. I'm pretty sure she reads all the postcards too and maybe even steams open personal mail. "Say hi to your folks, okay?"

"Sure," I said, staring at the box.

The return address said Brisbane. I sat on the bench outside and tore it open with my house key. Inside, a worn pair of Converse sneakers was nestled in a white T-shirt. I pulled out the T-shirt and held it up. It had Bugs Bunny on the front. I buried my face in it and inhaled, hoping to smell Lucky, but it smelled of laundry detergent. There was a note inside one of the shoes, just a few words, handwritten on a page raggedly torn from a lined notebook:

Thought you should have these things. Lucky left them with me when he stayed at my place for a few weeks. We're so sorry. We all miss him so much.

Love, Jennifer

I remembered Jennifer from Lucky's e-mails and photos, a pixie-haired girl with a gap in her front teeth and freckles. Lucky liked her a lot. I pulled the T-shirt on over the shirt I was wearing.

At the bottom of the box there was a book: *Blue-beard* by Kurt Vonnegut. I'd never heard of it.

I picked up the right sneaker and slid my hand inside it. I came out with a few grains of sand between my finger and thumb. Lucky's foot had been inside this sneaker, walking along a beach on the other side of the world. This *exact* sand had rubbed up against my brother's foot, maybe even irritated him as he walked. I let the grains fall away to the ground. Inside the left shoe was a small Swiss Army Knife. I put it back. I took the book and flipped it open to the title page. It was inscribed:

To Lucky,
I'm sorry. I meant no harm. Enjoy the book.
Your Evil Twin,
Fin

What had Fin done? Lucky was always very slow to anger and quick to forgive so it must have been something big, and signing it *Your Evil Twin*? What did he mean? There was nothing on the overleaf or even on the back describing the novel, but the first page was an author's note and the first line said:

"*This is a novel, and a hoax autobiography at that.*"

I pondered that as I sat huddled on the bench,

absentmindedly watching the post office comings and goings. I flipped through the pages of the book and stopped at a phone number written in a hurried scrawl across the top of the page. It definitely wasn't Lucky's handwriting. I wondered if Fin could have written it. The area code was 212. I dug out my phone and called the number. It rang several times and then a man picked up.

"Professor Hastings," said the voice.

I froze. Maybe this was an old number, written by a student.

"Hello?"

"Uh, who am I calling, please?"

"Professor Sam Hastings, NYU. Can I help you?"

"Oh. Hi. I might have the wrong number. This is a real long shot but do you happen to know someone named Fin?"

"No. Can't say I do."

My brain rushed ahead of me. "How about Abel Sacula?"

"Sure, I know Abe. Who is this?"

I thought fast. "Oh, um, my name's Georgia. Abel is a friend of my brother's and I'm planning a surprise birthday party. I wanted to invite him but I can't seem to find a number for him. A friend of my brother's told me you might be able to help me. He gave me your number. He didn't tell me you were a professor. I guess that's what threw me."

"Aw, gee. I have no idea where Abe could be. I haven't seen him in ages. He was friends with my younger brother, Kelly. They went to Julliard together. Actually, my dad knew him too. He runs an educational fund for foster kids. That's how they met. Abe won a scholarship."

My head started spinning. Was Kelly the boy on the boat in the photo?

"Tell you what. I'll give you my dad's number. He might be able to help you."

"That would be great," I said, rifling through my backpack for a pen.

He gave me his dad's name—Winston Hastings—and recited another New York number to me. I wrote it on the back of my hand.

"Thanks."

"Sure. Good luck. Say hi to Abe for me if you find him, okay?"

"I sure will. Thank you."

I kept the T-shirt on and put all the rest of the stuff from the box into my backpack. I pedaled along the highway toward my dad's oyster farm. I was buzzing with everything I'd learned in the last five minutes. Fin, formerly Abe, was somehow friends with a wealthy family in New York. What happened to that friendship? And he was in a foster home for enough time to get a scholarship? He hadn't mentioned that part of his story. I had an hour before I had to open up Katy's and I absolutely had to get there on time today. I'd been late opening the store the last few days and I'd missed a few Katy calls. I'd lied and told her I was in the bathroom, but it was wearing thin.

I hadn't been to the farm since that day my mom and dad and I took the boat out to scatter Lucky's ashes. I wasn't really sure why I was going today. It wasn't my intention when I left the house. My legs labored on the slight uphill grade of the road. I'd been so lazy about exercise for so long. The meds did that to me. I was excited at the prospect of getting in shape now.

The farm is not a particularly nice place to visit, especially not on a day with mounds of fog hovering close to shore even though it was mid-July. A brisk wind whipped my hair back from my face and forced tears from my eyes as I pedaled up the highway. My fingers and my ears were numb. I wished I'd worn gloves and a hat.

I turned into the drive and navigated around the potholes on the narrow dirt road. My dad's silver truck was side by side with Fin's red one, next to the shed.

Eduardo, the delivery truck driver, was power washing the oysters that were to be delivered later today. He waved. I leaned my bike against my dad's truck and looked out onto the estuary. My dad and Fin were out in the boat, pulling up seed cages to check the size of the oysters. Oysters grow at different rates so you have to manually pick out the ones that are market size and put the rest back in the water to mature. Both men were dressed in yellow waterproof overalls and long, heavy gloves. They had wool beanies on their heads. Fin must have been wearing Lucky's gear. Their laughter traveled across the water. My dad was teaching Fin the oyster business. They still hadn't seen me and I almost didn't want them to. I went to the shed and took my dad's binoculars off the hook by the door. I sat down at the wooden picnic table, which was coated in seagull poop. The fog was creeping closer and closer to shore. It blew across the storm-colored water like soft cotton balls. I turned the dial on the binoculars till my dad and Fin came into focus. The way Fin looked so sincere out there with my dad, so eager to learn, made me feel foolish about all the doubts I'd been having. I watched him laugh at a baby crab dangling from the index finger of his glove. He looked more appealing than ever.

My dad was showing Fin how to measure an oyster. He used the little metal ruler that he carries with him everywhere. He put the ruler in his pocket and pulled out his shucking knife. My dad can get an oyster from shell to mouth faster than anyone. He pulled the top half off the bottom shell and expertly loosened the muscle that attaches the oyster to the smooth pearly inside. He handed it to Fin, who tipped it back into his mouth like he'd been eating oysters all his life. Maybe he had. Fin's eyes closed and he smiled. My dad opened another oyster for himself. My binoculars drifted over to the right of them, toward the pier where the boat and stacks of seed cages are kept. I dropped the binoculars onto the rocks. I had to be seeing things. Was that Lucky sitting on the pier? Fog drifted over the dark, wet boards, blurring him for a few seconds, but when it passed I was certain I was looking at my brother. He seemed to be looking at exactly what I'd been looking at. I kept my eyes on him and reached to the ground for the binoculars. I quickly trained them on the pier again. Lucky was still there. He was sitting cross-legged on the wet boards. His favorite beach towel was wrapped around him, the one with the multicolored stripes. I stood up.

"Lucky! Over here!" I called out to him. I waved

and jumped up and down, but he didn't see me. Maybe it was the fog, which was almost on shore now. I ran to the edge of the water, calling out to him again. I was up to my thighs in icy-cold water. My dad and Fin were trying to see me through the fog. I pointed at the pier.

"It's Lucky. Look! It's Lucky!"

They looked over to where I was pointing. I pushed off the slippery bottom rocks with my sneakers and started swimming toward the pier. I was still screaming Lucky's name and choking and sputtering. My dad started the boat's motor and steered it toward me. I could tell by the look on his face that he didn't see what I saw. My clothes were heavy and waterlogged now and pulling me under. My legs were frozen; I couldn't move them at all. My head dipped below the surface, and I opened my eyes. Lucky was four feet from my face. His hair was splayed out around his head and his eyes were bulging out in panic. He looked exactly like he did in my nightmares. The striped towel was behind him in the water, moving like a colorful sea creature through the turbulence. Lucky reached out to me. I groped the water, trying to take his hands in mine, but I needed to get closer. I tried to kick my legs but they were numb. The last thing I remember before everything went dark was a strong arm reaching into the water for me. Fin's hand grabbed mine. He was grabbing the same hand I'd just written Winston Hastings's number on in black ink. Then I was pulled up and out and away from Lucky.

TWENTY

I woke up alone in a bed in a small room. I was wearing a hospital gown. It seemed to be nighttime.

I heard hospital noises from out in the hallway, doctors being paged, carts being rolled. I couldn't remember exactly how I'd gotten there. I couldn't see very well and I wondered what had happened to my contact lenses. I imagined them lying at the bottom of the estuary like tiny jellyfish. With a start I realized that I'd never gotten back to open Katy's.

I remembered being underneath my dad's heavy canvas coat as his truck bumped along. I was soaking wet and shivering so hard that my teeth were chattering. My dad kept glancing over at me. He looked worried. It had been a long time since he'd seen me do something crazy. I must have scared the hell out of him. I vaguely remember him calling my mom on his cell, instructing her to call Dr. Saul.

I tried to remember everything that had happened at the farm. If my dad and Fin hadn't pulled me out of the water I could have touched Lucky's hands. I wasn't imagining it. He was there. He was *that* close to me.

I ran my fingers through my hair. It was sticky with sea salt and hung in ropes. My body felt stiff and heavy, like I was still underwater. The door opened and my parents appeared. I felt sheepish when they smiled at me and asked me how I was feeling.

"Fine," I said. "I'm sorry." The grim look in their eyes was familiar. It had started appearing when I was nine and they were called to the school for the first time. There had been an incident. During dodgeball, which I loathed, Penny Michaelson threw a ball at me hard. She aimed for my head. She hated me. It hit my cheek with a sharp slap and jerked my head to the side, making my ears ring. My glasses flew off my face and hit the floor, shattering into pieces. The sting of embarrassment when everyone laughed was far worse than the sting on my cheek. I was a constant irritation in class. They were glad I was hurt. I put my hand to my face and felt a hot welt rising. I scurried underneath the wooden bleachers like a wounded animal. The gym emptied out and everyone went back to homeroom.

Mr. Ligetti, our gym teacher, tried to coax me out, but I stayed there under the bleachers, rocking and weeping. I knew that the whole school was talking about me. This was something I would never live down. I felt so ashamed. Finally, after two hours, my mom showed up. She crawled under the bleachers in her skirt and sandals and talked quietly to me. She took me home. That was the first of many "episodes," and though my parents wanted to believe that I was just going through a phase, I knew better. I wasn't like anyone else in my class and I never would be. I couldn't do the work. I couldn't focus. I couldn't play nicely with other kids. Our family doctor, Dr. Garcia, put me on Ritalin then and I was labeled a weird kid.

My mom and dad stood on opposite sides of my bed. My dad was still wearing his work clothes. My mom dug through her bag and handed me my glasses. I put them on.

"Are you okay?" she asked.

"I know you probably don't believe me, but I saw Lucky."

My mom patted my arm. "Of course you did, honey. The mind is a powerful thing." Her eyes pleaded *Please don't get weird on us again.*

"No, it wasn't my mind. He was sitting on the

pier. He was watching Dad and . . . Fin. Mom, he looked *so* scared."

My mom and dad exchanged glances.

"Look, I'll prove it. He had that big striped towel wrapped around him, his favorite. Remember that one? He dropped it in the water. I saw it there when I went under. Promise me you'll look for it at home. It's not there. I know it." They looked at me with pity.

"Please believe me," I said softly. "I saw him."

A nurse came in and gave me a shot of something. My eyes started to close. I fell into a deep, dreamless sleep. I slept like this, on and off, for what seemed like days, but it couldn't have been. I surrendered easily. I was drawn to the mindless, painless, beautiful floating feeling that the drugs brought. When I woke up the room was dim. It must have been nighttime again. The drapes were pulled closed and the light above my bed was on. Fin was standing over me. He pulled up a chair and sat down next to my bed. "I've been looking for you."

My heart started pounding. "What are you doing here?" I asked.

He ignored me. "So, you finally ended up in the loony bin." He looked around the room. "Well, I can't say I'm surprised. This place is hilarious, though.

There's a guy wandering around the hallway who thinks he's still in the Vietnam War."

He squeezed my forearm in his hand. "You've gotten so thin, like a sad little bird."

I yanked my arm away.

"You poor thing."

"What do you want?"

He leaned in close to my face. "You might think you know something, but you don't; it's all in your head, and if you're smart you'll keep it there. Anyway, it's not like anyone will believe you if you start chirping, especially now that you took a swim in the estuary." He laughed. "That looked pretty crazy." He stroked my cheek.

My eyes filled with tears. I looked away from him.

"Poor, poor Georgia."

"Get away from me."

"I bet they give you shock treatments."

"No. They won't."

"We'll see about that."

He stood up slowly and carefully put the chair back in its place. He started to leave.

"Why'd you have to kill him?" I asked. "Why couldn't you just be his friend?"

He turned back to me slowly and smiled. "Why would I want to be his friend when I could be *him*?

And you know what? It wasn't even that hard. Oh, and before I forget." He pulled something out of his inside jacket pocket. "This is from Lucky." He placed the necklace with the fearlessness charm on the metal table next to my bed. "He wanted you to have it."

Then he leaned over and whispered in my ear, "You're going to be quiet from now on, right?" He looked at me menacingly, inches from my face. His hair touched my cheek. I slowly nodded. He kissed me hard on my lips. "That's a good birdie," he whispered, and he was gone.

When I woke up again the room was bright. The drapes were open and sunlight streamed in. A nurse stood next to my bed. She smiled at me.

"Hello. How are you feeling?"

I looked over at the bedside table. The necklace was gone.

"Did you see a necklace?" I asked the nurse.

"Where?"

"On the table. A black cord with a silver charm?"

"No, Sweetie, I'm sorry. I didn't see it."

"Has anyone been in my room?" I asked

"No one but me," she said.

TWENTY ONE

On Sunday, two days after I was released from the hospital, I was feeling well enough to go to the Heron. When I went to get my backpack off the hook by the door, it wasn't there. Then I remembered that I'd left it on the picnic table at the oyster farm.

"Dad, have you seen my backpack?" I asked, loathing that I had to remind him of that day.

He looked up from reading the newspaper. "Don't think so. Where did you see it last?"

"The farm, on the picnic table."

"It'll turn up. Eduardo probably put it in the shed."

When I arrived at the Inn, I went to the pantry to get my work clogs and my apron. Someone had squeezed my backpack into my cubbyhole. I pulled it out and sat down on the floor. I dumped the contents out and did a quick inventory. My wallet, Lucky's shoes, the Swiss Army Knife, the book, and my phone—everything was there. I fanned through the Vonnegut book. Jennifer's note fell out and drifted to the floor. I looked for the page with the phone number. I found the spot. The number was still there. I opened my phone and turned it on. A sliver of battery life was left, but the phone had been fully charged just before I dropped it in my backpack on the way to Katy's. I went to the list of recent calls. Professor Hastings's number in New York was still there. I looked at the back of my hand. There was no sign of Winston Hastings's number left, but Fin had to have seen it when he pulled me out of the water. I knew that Fin was the one who put my backpack in the cubbyhole and that he'd looked at my phone. He knew that I'd made that call.

A big bowl of strawberries sat on the prep table. Each one of them was perfectly shaped and a deep-red color. I took the first one off the pile. I hulled it and started slicing it for the strawberry rhubarb tarts I had planned for that night's featured dessert. The heavy knife made a satisfying *tap-tap-tap* sound on the wooden cutting board. But I was distracted. Lucky's face at the estuary, the terrible fear in his eyes, was always there, the minute I went inside my head. I couldn't get him out of my mind.

My mom and dad had made it very clear that I would be seeing Dr. Saul regularly now. No more missed appointments. I agreed to go, but I had no intention of going back on my meds: Lucky was trying to tell me something, and if I went back to being medicated I'd never know what it was. I'd spent some time over the last couple days weighing out what was real and what was not. I saw Lucky at the oyster farm. He was real. But then had I seen Fin in the hospital? Was that real? His sinister-looking face, inches from mine, threatening me, certainly *seemed* real. And I could still feel his lips pressed against mine. There was no necklace, though.

I rinsed the leggy pink rhubarb stalks in the sink. Out the kitchen window I watched Fin's truck pull up into the gravel driveway that runs next to the kitchen garden, as though I'd conjured him. The bed of his old truck was loaded down with plants and shrubs and bags of soil. Almost immediately, Miles and Jeff appeared outside. Fin seemed to be describing the beautiful garden he was about to create for them. I could see Miles and Jeff visualizing it, giddy with anticipation. Fin was wearing his newsboy cap and a black short-sleeved T-shirt over a gray long-sleeved T-shirt. His jeans were torn at the knee and his olive skin peeked through. There was a pair of worn leather gloves stuffed into one of his pockets. The three of them were acting like old friends. The passenger door of the truck opened and Sonia got out. She was sipping a take-out coffee. Her lipstick left a dark-red smudge on the plastic lid. She wore large, delicate silver hoops in her ears, which made her look especially French. When she met Fin's eyes there was no doubt in my mind that she was in love with him.

I wanted to talk to Sonia more than ever, but this was not the time. I would have to wait till I could get her alone. Suddenly Rocket poked his head out of the driver's side of the truck. He was also in love with Fin. I felt an overwhelming wave of loneliness wash over me. I'd lost Lucky, I barely saw Sonia, and now even Rocket had abandoned me. Everyone I loved thought of me as unhinged.

I went back to my work at the prep table, bearing down on the knife to cut through the first rhubarb stalk. I gasped as it sliced through the tip of my index finger. Pain shot through my hand. I rushed back to the sink and ran cold water on it. I watched the blood swirl down the drain. With my good hand I grabbed the metal first aid kit from above the stove. I gently dried my finger on a paper towel. Blood still seeped out of the cut. I opened the disinfectant with my teeth and dabbed some on, yelping when it soaked in. Karl, who'd been out in the storeroom, arrived back in the kitchen carrying a bag of potatoes.

"Holy shit! How'd you do that?" He dropped the bag on the floor.

"It wasn't Plan A," I said. "Can you help me bandage it?"

"Nasty," he said, as he tore the wrapping off the biggest bandage in the kit and carefully wound it around my finger. "Too tight?"

I shook my head.

"Hold it up in the air. It'll slow the bleeding."

I took some deep breaths and watched out the window with my throbbing hand held up in the air. Fin and Sonia looked over at me. They thought I was waving at them. They waved back.

"That Fin guy's kind of cool," said Karl, standing next to me, watching out the window. "Who's that girl?"

"Sonia," I said abruptly. The pain in my finger was becoming unbearable.

"That's Sonia? Did she get a makeover?"

I rolled my eyes and walked away.

I headed to Katy's and arrived late again. A couple of tourists were on the porch, reading the hours posted on the door and then looking at their watches like mimes. I apologized to them. They actually had the nerve to look disappointed that they'd had to wait, like I was Amtrak or something. I unlocked the door and turned off the alarm.

Sharona pulled up, looking surprised to see me there. She went inside and helped the tourists while I hung the kites outside. While I was doing that I realized I'd forgotten our coffees too.

"Hey, great glasses," said Sharona, when I came back inside.

"Thanks."

Sharona said nothing about my absence over the last few days and I didn't bother trying to explain anything to her. Several messages from Katy's number were on my phone when I found it this morning but I'd deleted them. *My dead brother seemed to be trying to tell me something* probably wouldn't fly with her as an excuse for missing work.

Sharona looked at my hand. "What happened?"

The blood had seeped through the first bandage so I'd piled a few more on.

"Kitchen accident."

"Does it hurt?" She pulled the change bag out of the safe and unzipped it.

"Yeah, a lot. It's throbbing."

"Take ibuprofen. Have you got some?"

"No."

"I might." Sharona dug through her purse until she found two tablets at the bottom. She blew the lint off them and presented them to me. "A bit dusty but they should work." She brought me a glass of water from the bathroom.

I swallowed the painkillers and tasted Sharona's perfume in my mouth.

"Hey, do you believe in ghosts?" I asked, knowing that Sharona was definitely someone who would.

Without looking up from the cash drawer, she held up her index finger and finished counting a stack of dollar bills before she answered me.

"Believe in ghosts? Hell, yes. Have I not told you the story about my great-granny Dotty?"

I shook my head.

"She died in her bedroom on the second floor of our house. My mom was taking care of her. Dotty was ninety-seven and mostly blind and all she did all day was listen to gospel music on an old radio in her room. She used to spray Yardley English Rose perfume everywhere. Anyway, my bedroom is right above that room where she died and sometimes I wake up in the middle of the night and I can hear gospel music coming up through the floor and guess what I always smell?

"English Rose?" I said.

"That's right. Totally freaky."

"But did you ever see her ghost, like, in person?"

"Well, I never did but my mom swore she did. She claims she used to see great-granny Dotty wandering around in her favorite pale-blue nightgown all the time, but then my mom used to hit the sauce pretty hard, so you never know. I haven't heard much about Dotty's ghost since my mom got herself into AA." She finished counting out the change in the drawer and slid it under the cash register. "Now all she talks about is AA." She closed the cash drawer. "You got a ghost in your house? I know a woman who does séances. She's super-connected to the spirit world. She made these earrings." She touched a tiny silver angel dangling from her earlobe.

"I'll keep that in mind. Thanks. I was just wondering."

"Okay, well, just say the word." Sharona headed to the storeroom in the back to get taffy to restock the bins.

"We're out of piña colada!" she called out, "and banana!"

I made a note next to the register.

The phone rang half an hour later. Sharona picked it up. I could tell it was Katy by the way Sharona was talking. She was never herself when Katy called. Sharona glanced at me once while they spoke.

"Sure. She's right here." She handed me the phone with a grimace. "Brace yourself," she said.

I reluctantly took the phone. "Hello?"

"Hi, Georgia. How are you?" Katy had an officious way of talking that always made me nervous.

"Okay."

"Listen. I'm really sorry to have to tell you this but we've decided to let you go."

"Why?" I knew why.

"Well, we haven't been very pleased with your work lately. It's bad enough that you've been coming in late, but on Friday I had to drive out there and open the store myself."

I heard the twins screaming in the background. She covered the phone and I heard muffled yelling. "Brandon, Brandy, don't make me say it again!" I waited. "I'm sorry, what was I saying?"

"You were firing me."

"Right. Look, we'll put your paycheck in the mail. I'm sorry. I know this is a tough time for you with what happened to your brother and all—"

"Yeah, whatever."

I clicked the phone off and handed it to Sharona. "I guess I'm done here."

"That freaking uptight bitch. I knew she was up to something. What is her problem?"

"Me, I think. Problem solved."

"Hey, you want me to quit? I'll quit. This job sucks anyway."

"Nah. Don't worry about it. I don't even care."

I gathered up all my things: books, gum, sweaters, bandannas, sunglasses, a bike lock, magazines. Sharona followed me around the store bad-mouthing Katy, but I knew this wasn't really Katy's fault. I jammed everything into my backpack with Lucky's stuff and then I hugged Sharona. She held on to me tight and I felt tears prick at my eyes. It was likely I'd see her plenty, but still, I really liked this thing we had together. I would miss it a lot.

"I'm gonna fight to get your job back," she said, sniffing.

"Don't. I don't want it."

"And if she thinks I'm picking up your hours, she's delusional."

I put my backpack on and looked around.

"Take some taffy. Take as much as you want. I won't tell."

"No. Thanks." I walked out the door and my career in retail was over.

TWENTY TWO

Dr. Saul looked at my bandaged finger but he didn't comment.

"How are things?"

"Okay. I got fired from one of my jobs yesterday." Was it yesterday? Why couldn't I keep my days straight?

"Why?"

"I sucked at it."

"I'm sure that's not true."

"Well, I guess I don't really care that much."

"And you've lost some weight, I see."

Had I? Maybe. "I'm good. I feel good."

"How are you sleeping?"

"Fine. I guess. Sometimes. I'm not really tired."

"Georgia, are you back to taking two pills a day?"

I looked away. "Not exactly."

"Georgia, this is extremely dangerous, what you're doing. The dosage isn't for you to decide."

I said nothing for a couple of minutes. He watched me expectantly. It had never occurred to me before that he looked exactly like an owl.

"I've been feeling better."

"How so?"

"Stronger, sharper, smarter, more alert, more energetic. Everything is better. I can even *hear* better. I can hear conversations that other people are having across a room."

He looked at me gravely. "It's dangerous and irresponsible, what you're doing. You could have a schizophrenic episode at any time."

I scratched my cheek and looked out the window.

"Georgia?"

"What?"

"You need to go back on your meds. I had you admitted last Friday and I can admit you again if I feel that you're a danger to yourself."

I shook my head vigorously. "Dr. Saul, no offense, but you don't know the first thing about danger. *I* know danger. Believe me, I do. And guess what else? No headaches anymore. Poof! They're gone. And you know what else? I'm *not* scared, not at all." That was a lie. I scratched my scalp. I looked around the room. It felt smaller than before.

"Did you change this room? It looks different."

"What do you mean?"

"It's different. Like, smaller."

"No, Georgia, it's the same room."

"I could swear it's different."

"I'm going to have to talk to your parents again. I'm afraid I can't trust you. I'm sorry."

"Please don't do that."

"I wish I didn't have to. You've left me no choice."

I shrugged. "Fine. Tell them. They don't care anyway. They wish it was me who died instead of Lucky."

He sighed. "That isn't true."

I got up and picked up my backpack. "Well, I'm not taking my meds. Do whatever you have to. I don't care." Then I walked out of there.

TWENTY THREE

"Can I have this?" I dangled a lacy violet bra from my finger.

"Where did you find that?" Sonia snatched it out of my hand and tossed it onto the floor.

"Here." I held up her sweater. "It was in the pocket."

Sonia blushed. Rocket looked from me to her and back to me.

"Shut up."

"I didn't say anything."

Sonia hurled a throw pillow at me.

"Ow, careful." I held up my bandaged finger.

"What happened?"

"I was slicing rhubarb."

"Did it bleed a lot?" she asked. Sonia is squeamish about blood.

"Yes. I could have died."

She smiled.

"Where'd you get that shirt?" She looked at my Bugs Bunny T-shirt.

"Jennifer in Australia sent it to me. It was Lucky's."

"I know. There's a bloodstain on it."

"That's mine." I held up my finger again.

"Right."

"Katy fired me, by the way."

"She did? Why?"

I shrugged. "Doesn't matter. I hated working there."

Sonia looked concerned. "Are you okay?"

"Yes. I'm great."

I had come over to Sonia's place to talk to her as soon as I got home from Dr. Saul's, but I still hadn't quite found the words. Instead I lay next to her on her big bed. Rocket sighed and curled up on the braided rug on the floor. A framed photo of Sonia and Lucky, rosy-cheeked and smiling, sat on her bedside table. It looked like it was taken at a ski resort. Sonia saw me looking at it and her face became wistful. She looked up at the ceiling and we were quiet for a minute.

"So?" she faced me again.

"So what?"

"I hear you took a swim at the estuary."

"Yup."

"Are you okay? You wanna talk about it?"

"What did he tell you?"

"Fin?"

"No, Tom Cruise." I smirked at her.

"He said you . . . went a little crazy."

"Sonia, I saw Lucky . . . I . . ."

She interrupted me, shaking her head. "No. You didn't. Lucky's gone." I heard impatience creeping into her voice.

"I did, Sonia, I swear. He was right there on the pier."

"Look. I understand that you *think* you did, but it's hard for me to hear that from you. You know?" She rubbed my arm.

I rolled over and stared at the ceiling. "What happened in Australia?"

"What do you mean?"

"Something happened between the three of you. Was it when you took the trip to Sydney?"

She was quiet for a minute. "Who told you?"

"Jesse."

"But he didn't . . ."

"Look, I'm not stupid. I know that you were both

lying to me about how well you knew each other when Fin got here."

I looked over at her. A tear was rolling slowly down her cheek.

"Oh, God. You must think I'm a horrible person," she said.

"I don't think that at all."

She propped herself up on her elbow and looked at me. "You have to know that I had nothing to do with him coming here. I never thought I would see him again after Australia."

"Okay. What happened there?"

She sighed. "Lucky invited him along on our trip to Sydney. He didn't even ask me first. I was *so* angry. I wanted just the two of us to go on that trip. I'd worked every shift I could get at that shitty restaurant on campus to save for the flight and then I flew fourteen hours to get there and we'd been with his friends the whole time. I just wanted to take off for a few days alone before I flew home, you know?"

I nodded.

"I was really excited about it. But you know Lucky, always surrounded by people. So, he invited Fin along without asking me first, and the thing is, he barely knew him back then. So now we're in the car and it's the two of them talking surfing the whole way. I put on my headphones and listened to music and fumed. Lucky knew I was pissed but he didn't do anything about it."

She stopped talking. She was thinking a moment and then she said, "There's a reason I didn't tell you this story. I didn't want things to be weird between us. I felt ashamed because I loved Lucky so much. I still love Lucky. He's all I see when I close my eyes."

"Me too," I said. "Tell me the rest."

"We stopped in Coff's Harbor and checked into a cheap motel. We got the boards off the top of the car and went down to the beach. Conditions were good: medium swells, the size I like to ride best. I was surfing really well that day. I could see Fin watching me and I knew he was attracted to me, but, you know, whatever, I guess I was flattered. Lucky didn't even notice." She sighed. "That night we went to a bar in town. It was one of those noisy, crowded places, filled with young people, mostly surfers and tourists. We were squeezed together, shoulder to shoulder. Lucky was getting drunk. He'd already made friends with a pack of Aussies and I was left alone with Fin. He hung on every word I said and didn't even seem to notice anyone else in the bar. I'd had a few beers and I was getting a little drunk myself. The bar was hot and stuffy and I started feeling nauseous. I said I was going out for some air.

Fin came with me and we ended up walking down to the beach. I thought the fresh air would clear my head but it made me feel drunker."

She stopped. She looked pained. "Fin kissed me and I kissed him back. We started making out in the sand. It was just because I was drunk and I was so angry at Lucky." Tears appeared on her cheeks again. She wiped them away.

"So, I guess Lucky finally noticed we weren't in the bar and he started looking for us. And then he found us." She wiped her nose with the back of her hand.

"What did he do?"

"He looked like he couldn't believe what he was seeing, and then he looked as hurt as I'd ever seen him." Sonia sobbed. "And then he just walked away. The next morning we left the motel without Fin and drove the rest of the way to Sydney. I apologized over and over. I told him I was drunk, I told him I was mad, and he said it was okay, but I knew it wasn't. A few days later we said good-bye at the airport in Sydney and I flew home. Lucky had to drive back to Brisbane alone. It was the last time I saw him alive." She sniffed.

I thought about the video and about what Fin had written in the Vonnegut book. "But Fin was there the day Lucky died. Did Lucky forgive him?"

Sonia shrugged. "I don't know. I've never talked about it with Fin, or with Lucky, for that matter. I think we all wanted to forget that it happened."

I lay there thinking. Maybe that's why Sonia got so angry when I said I saw Lucky. She didn't even want the ghost of Lucky seeing her with Fin like this.

"I have to pee," I said, getting up off the bed.

I walked down the hall to the bathroom and closed the door. I sat down on the toilet seat. Something bright pink in the garbage next to the toilet caught my eye. I dipped my hand into the garbage and pulled it out carefully. It was an empty box from a pregnancy test. I sifted carefully through the tissues and Q-tips and makeup remover pads until I found it: a long, narrow shape wrapped carefully in toilet paper. I slowly unwrapped it, dreading what I would find, as the package got smaller and smaller. Finally I was staring at a plastic stick. The little window had two pink lines in it. Pregnant. Sonia was pregnant.

I hurriedly wrapped the stick up again and hid it at the bottom of the garbage and went back to Sonia's bedroom, trying to look calm while I was freaking out.

Sonia was staring up at the ceiling.

I heard a truck pull into the driveway and I knew it was Fin. Sonia sat up in the bed and looked out the window.

"Fin's here." She quickly wiped her eyes and patted her hair into place.

"I know," I said

Rocket jumped up and ran for the door.

"Do you love him?"

She hesitated. "Oh, George, don't make me answer that. Not today."

I tried to smile. "Okay."

"Hey, come with us. He's playing down in Point Reyes. Come, okay?"

"I can't. I got stuff to do."

I heard his pointy black boots on the porch steps and then he opened the back door. A flurry of fear ran down the back of my neck.

Sonia got up off the bed. I lay there, listening to Fin's voice as he talked to Rocket.

"Hey boy, whassup?" Rocket's nails click-clacked on the hardwood. He was dancing around in excited circles.

"Hey. What's wrong?" I heard him say softly. He must have noticed that Sonia's eyes were red from crying.

Sonia didn't speak but I knew they were kissing. I could hear them. Sonia laughed softly and Fin pushed her down the hallway and up against the wall next to her bedroom door where I could see them. Fin pressed himself up against her. Sonia's eyes drifted over to me. He followed her gaze. He seemed amused, seeing me there, watching them. He winked at me. He was wearing a gray cashmere sweater and a soft-looking wool scarf.

"Hey, George, how ya doin'?"

"She should come with us, shouldn't she?"

"Uh, definitely. You want to come with us, George?"

"No. Thanks."

On the porch Sonia hugged me and whispered that she would call me later. "I love you," she said. "I'm so sorry."

I clipped Rocket's leash on and we walked down the hill, toward the beach. Fin's truck came up behind us, and Sonia blew me a kiss as they drove by me.

TWENTY FOUR

After my visit with Sonia I started sleeping even less. When I did sleep, it was in short spurts and I had bad dreams. Sleep was not my friend anymore. Staying awake was safer. Besides, I didn't seem to need sleep. I wanted to be alert when Lucky came back. I wished he could just tell me what he wanted me to know, or what he wanted me to do. If I could just talk to him I could make a plan. I could get ready.

My mom was doing another wood firing in the backyard kiln. She was getting ready for a big show in Santa Fe. She'd started the fire early in the morning with a ceremonial match, a quick prayer to the fire gods, and some lighter fluid. She'd been feeding logs into the kiln all day.

From my bedroom window I could see sparks

shooting out from the chimney into the inky night sky. I fell onto my bed and though I was wide awake, my eyelids started to grow heavy. I guess I must have fallen asleep. When I woke up it felt like hours later. I was in Lucky's bed. I couldn't remember how I got there. I sat up and looked around the room. A great horned owl was sitting on Lucky's dresser, watching me. His eyes were a beautiful shade of amber. One eye lazily closed and opened again. He slowly stretched his massive wings out like an accordion and then drew them in again, shifting his white talons, which were clutching the edge of an open drawer. He made a strange jerking movement with his head, like there was something caught in his throat. He seemed to be gagging on something. He opened his beak wide and regurgitated a large egg-shaped pellet onto the floor beneath him. I stood up slowly and walked over to him. He stayed where he was, calmly watching me. I crouched down and picked up the pellet. It was warm and slimy. All the little white pills I had thrown out my bedroom window were tangled up inside a grey clump of hair and fur and tiny bones.

When I woke up I was back in my own bed again, but it was still dark out. I looked around my room for the owl but there was no sign of him. The house was cold. I wrapped a quilt around me, slid into my slippers, and walked into the kitchen. I put the kettle on for tea and went into Lucky's room. His bed was neatly made. I went over to the dresser. The open drawer that the owl had been perched on was shut. I saw something on the floor. I crouched down and picked it up. It was an owl feather, a small one, striped with a bit of downy fluff on the end. I brushed it against my cheek. Back in the kitchen I put the feather in an abalone shell on the counter. I stood at the window and watched the kiln burn. The kettle started to hiss. I filled a mug and dangled a tea bag in the water. I carried the mug with me out the back door. There was a damp chill in the air. I put my tea down and grabbed an armload of wood off the pile and dropped it in the sand next to the kiln. I opened the kiln door and the heat smacked me in the face.

I fed the pieces of wood in, one at a time. The fire was so hot that the pieces caught immediately. I loaded in piece after piece. I was standing there watching the flames lick up onto the wood when suddenly I got a tingly scalp feeling and I was certain that someone was standing behind me. I spun around and peered into the darkness.

"Is someone there?" I said. I couldn't see anything but I felt something or someone near me. I resisted the urge to reach out into the darkness for fear I might touch someone. I wrapped my quilt tighter around me and walked tentatively along the stone path that led past my mom's dark studio and out to the street. A moth beat itself against the glass porch light above the front door of the house. The moon was almost full, and it shed light onto the pavement. I looked up and down the quiet, empty street and then I noticed that the bushes along the side of the house were trembling though the air was perfectly still. Something had brushed past them seconds ago. I took a few steps till I could see all the way to the bottom of the hill. I thought I saw a shadow, a tall thin shadow, turn the corner and dart quickly across the Coast Highway and disappear.

The sky started to lighten to mauve as I made my way down the hill. Most of the houses in False Bay were still dark. Porch lights burned and smoke drifted lazily from the chimneys. The only sound I heard was my bedroom slippers slapping against the cracked pavement and the occasional car winding along the coast.

I don't know why I started walking down the side of the highway. I passed by the Heron and turned right at the small lane that led to Jeff and Miles's house. A dog barked off in the distance, but their street was quiet. I turned into the driveway and walked along the side of the house. I stopped suddenly. Fin was sitting cross-legged on a bench on the redwood deck. He had a beach towel wrapped around him. He sat perfectly still, facing the water. I quickly backed up and ducked behind a small tree. Soft light glowed through the red-and-white-checkered curtains that hung in the windows of the redwood cottage at the back of the property.

Fin looked off to his right and my heart raced, thinking he may have sensed me watching him. He dropped the towel and hopped off the edge of the deck. He walked toward a stand of old redwoods and stopped next to the biggest one, gazing up into the branches. He stayed that way for what seemed like minutes and then he turned and headed toward me. I darted behind Jeff's SUV and crouched down. Fin walked over to his truck, which was parked right next to Jeff's in the driveway. He rooted around in the truck bed and came out with an armful of heavy rope. He opened the truck door and took the hunting knife out of the glove box. He put it in his back pocket and headed back toward the tree. I returned to my spot and crouched down again. Fin took aim and threw a heavy coil of rope up and over the thickest limb with ease. He caught it as it fell. He pulled the knife out of his pocket and sawed through the rope and threw the remaining rope over the limb, a few feet closer to the trunk. He looked around and then he walked over to the metal storage shed where the lawn mower is kept. He went inside and came out with an old tire under his arm and walked back over to the tree. He wrapped both ropes around the tire and then expertly knotted them. He climbed inside the tire, testing it with his weight, and then he swung back and forth like a child, his legs straight out in front of him. He was smiling. He seemed delighted with himself. The sun was starting to come up now and it filtered through the redwood branches. He untangled himself from the swing and jogged back toward the cottage. He was in there for a while and I was starting to think I should get out of there when he reappeared in the doorway with Sonia ahead of him, blindfolded with her own green scarf. She was wearing an oversized T-shirt and pajama bottoms. He guided her from behind with his hands on her shoulders, over toward the tree.

"This better be good, Fin," she laughed. He caught her by her elbows when she stumbled.

"How much farther?"

"Ten feet, almost there."

He pulled off the blindfold. She looked at the swing and squealed with delight.

"You made this for me?"

"Yes, get on." He held it steady while she climbed

in and he pushed her from behind, higher and higher. She tipped back and let her long hair dangle down. She squealed like a little kid. I felt an awful ache watching them. I felt like a bitter, jealous troll. I got up and walked down the drive. I looked back once more before I started up the street. Fin was looking in my direction. He'd seen me. He slowly lifted a hand and waved.

TWENTY FIVE

"Hey, are you okay?" Jeff examined my face.

"Yeah, sure."

" 'Cause you look sort of . . . flimsy."

"I'm fine." I tapped my sneaker impatiently. I had things to do.

"And Miles said he saw you walking away from our place early this morning. He said you were wrapped in a quilt and wearing bedroom slippers."

"I was out for a walk."

"Really? A walk? At six a.m.?"

I sighed heavily. "Yeah, I'm a morning person now but I haven't quite got the wardrobe worked out."

He cocked his head at me and looked confused.

"So, you said you wanted to talk to me?" I squinted

at the morning sun streaming in through the tall din-ing room windows. The bright light felt like an assault to me. Inn guests sat at the tables, enjoying breakfast. Cutlery clattered on plates. I felt raw and exposed.

"Yeah, sit down."

I reluctantly pulled out a chair and sat.

"Muffy is moving to Santa Barbara," he said, tak-ing a sip of his coffee. "Her mom is sick."

"Who's Muffy?"

"Muffy is the woman who supplies the Heron with breakfast muffins," he said.

"You mean Maureen?"

"I thought her name was Muffy."

"No one on earth is named Muffy. Her name is Maureen."

"But her muffin company is called Muffy's Muffins."

"I know."

"Okay, anyway, Miles and I were wondering if you could make the muffins from now on."

"I don't know if I can make them like she can." Actually, I'd never baked a muffin in my life. I wasn't sure if I could handle more baking. I immediately started to feel anxious.

"That's just it. We don't want you to. We want our

own muffins, something a bit less sugary, and smaller, and maybe more breakfasty, you know, like a signature muffin?"

I imagined Miles and Jeff lying on their 400-thread-count sheets discussing what they'd like to see in the way of Heron Inn signature muffins.

"Uh, I guess I could try out a few recipes. When do you need these by?"

"Yesterday. We aren't even getting a delivery from Muffy this week."

"Maureen."

"Whatever. Anyway, her mom was rushed to the hospital with a stroke or something like that." He waved his hand dismissively, like he was annoyed at the inconvenient timing of Maureen's mom's stroke.

"Okay," I said reluctantly.

"Beautiful. Why don't you make a few different ones and Miles and I will taste them. Oh, and we *love* morning glories. Maybe you could try making some of those?"

What's a morning glory?

I did a little online muffin research and then rode Lucky's bike to the market to scrounge up some ingredients for the test muffins. Before I left the Inn, Jeff gave me forty dollars, wincing at having to pay retail.

He made sure to remind me to get a receipt and to bring him his change, as though I might leave town with all forty of his dollars. I'd already printed out several recipes, but I decided to make one muffin that would be available year-round—banana-walnut—and one seasonal one.

I was examining a Gravenstein apple in the produce section when I spied Sonia heading briskly for the checkout.

"Hey!" I called out to her.

She turned around. She looked slightly alarmed to see me here. "Oh, hi, George. How's it going?"

"It's going. Whatcha doing?"

"Nothing much." She shifted nervously. She put her shopping basket down on the floor. There was nothing in the basket but soda crackers and 7 UP. "Man, are you okay? You look like shit."

"I'm just a little tired," I said. But I wasn't tired. Not at all. And anyway, she was looking a little green herself. I wondered when she was going to tell me that she was pregnant. Why would she keep it from me? Maybe Fin told her not to tell anyone yet.

"What are you making?" she asked, looking at my basket of muffin ingredients.

"Muffins, for the Inn."

"What about Maureen?"

"She's in Sacramento, er, no, Santa Barbara. Her mom is sick."

"Oh, that's too bad. I like her muffins."

"Jeff and Miles want me to create a signature muffin for the Inn." I rolled my eyes.

"Yeah, well, they would, wouldn't they?"

She looked at me more closely now, forgetting her hurry. "Hey, seriously, are you okay?"

"Yes, I wish people would stop asking me that."

"Are you eating?"

I shrugged.

Sonia looked at the door. "Well, I should probably run. My mom needs milk for her tea. You know how she gets. "

"Sure, yeah, okay." But there was no milk in her basket.

"Let's get together soon. Call me later, okay?" I saw worry in her eyes when she looked at me again.

"You bet," I said, but I wanted to say, *Please, stay here and talk to me some more. Tell me what's going on.*

She rushed over to the checkout and waved at me as she flew out the door with a paper bag in her arms. I watched her jump into the passenger side of Fin's truck. From where he was parked, he would have seen our whole exchange. He watched me watching them, and he smiled.

I put the apple back with the others.

I decided that I would bake the muffins at night after the staff at the Heron had all cleared out. That way I'd have the kitchen to myself. I never slept anyway. I tried to tell myself that it wasn't affecting me, but I felt wrung out and heavy-limbed. Every move I made seemed like a huge effort. Even pulling on my jeans exhausted me. The dark circles around my eyes looked like bruises. My nerves were frayed. I was anxious all the time. I constantly jumped at loud noises and even the quietest music bugged me. I never realized before how much my parents talked to each other. It was a constant stream of chatter that I couldn't tune out.

When I arrived at the Inn later that night, the dining room was empty and the kitchen staff was almost finished cleaning up. Marc was at the bar, wiping down his precious knives and sliding them into their leather case. I heard Fin's voice at the bar too. He and Marc were having an after-shift beer and speaking French. I stayed in the kitchen and kept quiet. I was certain that they hadn't seen me come in. I set the oven temperature and started in on the banana-walnut batter. I could hear bits of their conversation. Marc seemed to be talking about a restaurant he worked at in Manhattan.

"*Vous êtes jamais allés a New York?*" he asked Fin.

I know enough French to understand that he asked Fin if he'd been to New York.

"*Si,*" said Fin

Si? *That's it? Not, "I went to school there" or "I lived there"?*

I slowly mixed the dry ingredients into the wet.

"*C'est fantastique, n'est-ce pas?*" asked Marc.

"*Oui, fantastique. Mais très cher.*"

"*Oui, c'est sur.*"

I heard the sound of a barstool scraping across the wooden floor. I poured the batter into the industrial muffin tins and slid the first pan into the oven. That lie had appeared so easily. Why would Fin not want Marc to know he'd lived in New York? Had he told me all that stuff so that I would feel a bond with him, or did he do it to encourage me to share my vulnerable side with him so he could use it against me later?

"*Eh bien, je m'en vais, mon ami,*" said Marc.

"*Attendez une minute, je sors avec vous.*"

It sounded like he told Marc he'd walk out with him.

I dashed into the pantry and stood perfectly still. The two of them walked through the kitchen, and then their voices echoed down the hallway to the staff exit of the restaurant. I heard Marc's car start up. I walked back into the kitchen and saw his headlights through the window as he drove off. Fin's shadowy figure strolled on foot up the road away from the Inn. Except for the hum of the walk-in, the kitchen was dead quiet.

I started on the second batch of batter for pumpkin-orange muffins. I was having trouble focusing and I had to keep rereading the recipe. I cracked the eggs into a big bowl, added brown sugar, vanilla, and oil, and measured out the dry ingredients.

I had just opened a can of pumpkin and started zesting some oranges into a small glass bowl when I heard an odd noise—probably one of the guests upstairs. I walked into the darkened dining room and stood there listening. It was quiet. I went back to the kitchen and checked the muffins in the oven, then returned to my batter. I heard the noise again, closer this time. It wasn't coming from the guest rooms above me. It was definitely coming from the ground floor. Maybe a guest had forgotten their key. It happened all the time. I walked through the swinging kitchen doors and back out into the hallway, toward the small front lobby. I stopped in my tracks. My heart jolted and started thumping in my chest. Lucky was standing behind the oak desk. He had a drawer open. He was looking for something. He was wearing his wetsuit, and there were foot-shaped puddles of water from the front door to where he was standing now. A surfboard leash was fastened around his ankle, the end of it raggedly cut. He pulled a pen out of the drawer.

"Lucky?" I called softly.

He didn't look up for a few seconds, and then suddenly he lifted his head but he looked right past me. His eyes were filled with fear. He seemed to be looking at something over my shoulder. I spun around. Fin was leaning up against the wall with his arms crossed, watching me. "Boo!" He laughed.

I frowned at him.

"Boy, you look bad, Georgie. Is everything okay? Remember when you looked just like Lucky? Now you look *Un*-Lucky." He smirked.

"What are you doing here?"

"I was about to ask you the same thing."

"I'm working."

"You don't look like you're working. You look like you're skulking around the hallways."

"I heard a noise."

He walked past me and casually opened a drawer in the oak desk in the foyer, the same drawer that Lucky had just been looking through. He pulled out a set of keys and jangled them for me to see.

"Forgot my keys. I've started locking the cabin."

He walked past me again. I looked at the keys dangling from a ring on his index finger. One of them was long and slender and old, like the type of key you might use to open the drawer of an old dresser.

"Oh, and George?" he looked back over his shoulder at me.

"Yeah?"

"Don't stay here alone too late. This place is full of things that go bump in the night."

As soon as Fin was gone, I rushed over to where Lucky had been standing. I waved my arms around, trying to find him, or at least *feel* him. There was a small puddle of water on the floor behind the desk. I crouched down and touched my finger to it. I tasted it—salty. The footprint-shaped puddles of water that led all the way to the Inn's front door were still there. On the desk, there was a notepad. In shaky writing were the words *STOP HIM*. I stared at the notepad. Drops of water on the page blurred the words. I tore the page off the pad and stuffed it into my pocket. I started back to the kitchen to pull my muffins out of the oven, but halfway down the hallway I stopped. I slid down the wall to the floor. I couldn't go any further. I sobbed into my knees.

TWENTY SIX

Dr. Saul watched me. I squirmed in my chair.

"Are you feeling anxious?" he asked.

"No," I said. I was more terrified than anxious but I couldn't tell him that. Anyway, the fear would pass. I just had to trust Lucky. Lucky would tell me what to do.

"Would you like me to write you a prescription? Something to help you sleep?"

"No. Thanks. I don't want to sleep."

"Why not? Aren't you tired? You look exhausted."

I was more tired than I'd ever been in my life. "I'm tired and I'm wired," I said.

"But if I sleep, I could miss him."

"Him? You mean Lucky?"

"Yes, of course I mean Lucky. We're working together. He's working through me."

"What do you mean 'through you'?"

"He's dead but he's still here. He's communicating with me. Most of the time he's in my head and sometimes he's right there in front of me. He tells me things." I pulled the crumpled, smeared note from my pocket and smoothed it on my leg. I held it up. "He wrote me this note."

He leaned forward and squinted, reading the note. "Stop ham?"

"Stop him. It says *Stop him*."

"Where did you find that?"

"At the Inn."

"Are you sure someone who works at the Inn didn't write it? Maybe it's in regard to a delivery. It looks like it says ham. Did you ask the kitchen staff?"

I glared at him and refolded the note. He sat back in his chair and adjusted his glasses.

"Where is Lucky now?"

"He's right here, well, not in this room, not this second, anyway." I looked around quickly. My eyes stung. My head felt too heavy for my body.

"Please listen to me carefully, Georgia. What you're experiencing are delusions related to your illness. I know that these episodes seem very real to you, but please try to understand that your reality has shifted. I promise you that they will only get worse and more frequent if you aren't getting the proper treatment and meds. It's very dangerous: the not sleeping, the weight loss, the manic behavior. It's all part of it. I'm recommending hospitalization for you until we get this under control again."

"The hospital again? Don't be ridiculous, Dr. Saul. I'm fine."

"I'm afraid that's not true, Georgia."

"I found a belt in Lucky's dresser that I'm wearing so my jeans won't fall down. Look, it's Indian beaded along the back to say Montana." I stood up and turned around to show him. "See?"

He went back to writing furiously on his pad. I'd become much more interesting lately, scribble-worthy. What the hell was he writing?

I looked out the window at my mom's car in the drive. She sat slumped at the wheel, smoking, staring gloomily at the alpacas. Poor Mom.

"Did you hear what I said, Georgia? I'm going to . . ."

"Yes! I heard you the first time and the answer is no. I won't go. And I'm pretty sure you can't make me, I mean, legally."

"Actually, I can."

I could see his anger bubbling up. He took a deep breath and exhaled slowly, composing himself. I tried to think of something to say that would put his mind at ease, something that would make him realize that he was overreacting.

"I have it together, Dr. Saul. This is what I'm like when I'm working on something important."

He looked doubtful again.

"Stop looking at me like that."

"Like what?"

"Like I'm crazy. You're supposed to be helping me."

"I'm trying to help you."

"By locking me up? Not helpful, Dr. Saul, not helpful at all."

"Okay, Georgia, how can I help you? *You* tell *me*."

I tried to put into words what I wanted to say to him. It was so difficult now that everything came to me so randomly. My mind was jumbled but my thoughts were as sharp as shards of glass. That was the payoff. I was sharp. I *saw* everything. I certainly wasn't going to tell Dr. Saul that. I couldn't go back on the meds. Not now. Not when I was so close to knowing the whole story.

"Georgia?"

"I'm thinking."

Nights had become the hardest for me. I'd started

making a habit of walking over to Jeff and Miles's house. I sat in the dirt by the side of the garage, watching the little redwood cottage. I tried to remember to bring a blanket. If I forgot, the cold from the ground would crawl up through my bones and I would start to shiver. Bugs attacked me. Sometimes a light burned in the window through the checkered curtains and sometimes Fin would be sitting on the deck with his blanket wrapped around him. I watched him. He watched the water.

"Georgia?"

"What?"

"When did you last see Lucky?"

"The other day, in the lobby at the Heron. It was close to midnight. He was looking for something. Afterward there was saltwater on the floor where he'd been standing. I tasted it. And then I found the note."

"The Heron is a block off the ocean. Couldn't one of the guests have dripped saltwater on the floor?"

"No," I said impatiently. "It was foggy and cold that day. No one would have gone in the water."

He wrote something on his pad.

"What were you doing at the Heron at midnight?"

"Baking muffins," I told him. "Legitimate business."

But I'd forgotten to take the muffins out of the oven. After Fin left I sat on the wooden floor in the hallway with my back against the wall for what seemed like hours. I was paralyzed. When I finally got up, my legs were shaking and I was dizzy. I ran for the ladies' room and vomited. Then I curled up beside the toilet on the cool tile floor and traced the honeycomb pattern with my finger. By the time I pulled the muffins from the oven they were scorched on top. I had to throw them away. I didn't care about muffins anymore. I didn't really care much about anything except Lucky and uncovering the truth.

"If you want to help me, I need you to take me seriously."

"I do, Georgia."

"Dr. Saul, I'm pretty sure my brother was murdered."

"Well, I'm not surprised. It's consistent with the delusions you've been having."

He hadn't even considered what I'd said. He shook his head like he pitied me. I regretted telling him anything. Maybe I finally needed to say it out loud to someone. I'd been carrying it around with me for some time now. But Dr. Saul was obviously not the person I should be talking to about this.

"Oh, I almost forgot," he said. He got up and pulled open a drawer on his desk. He held up the necklace with the fearlessness charm. I stared at it, frozen.

"Is it yours?"

I nodded slowly.

"The hospital gave it to me. They found it on the floor behind the bedside table, and they asked me to return it to you. One of the nurses said you were looking for it."

I took it from him. "Thanks," I said. I didn't want my face to betray what I was feeling. I got out of there as fast as I could.

My mom was on her cell, talking to Dr. Saul, obviously. I stood there, clutching the necklace. I looked around. I considered taking off. I could just run into the woods from here. I obviously wasn't safe. I was still thinking about it when my mom leaned out the window. "Georgia, get in the car," she said. I got in. She looked anxious.

I watched out the window and trembled all the way back to my house.

TWENTY SEVEN

As soon as I got home from Dr. Saul's I went into my room and called Sonia. "Can I come over?" I asked. "I need to talk to you right away."

"Sure, I have something I want to tell you too."

My stomach dropped.

"Where are you going?" my mom asked as I took Rocket's leash from a hook at the door and whistled for him.

"Sonia's."

"I think you should stay home. I . . ."

"No." I darted out the door on shaky legs.

We walked down the hill to Sonia's. I realized I'd forgotten a jacket. When Sonia opened the door, Rocket charged around her house, looking for Fin, whose scent was probably everywhere. Sonia looked different. Besides the burgundy hair and the bright red lips, I couldn't quite put my finger on what was different about her. And then I remembered that she was pregnant.

"Are you okay?" she asked. "You're shaking."

"No. Can we go down to the beach?"

"Sure. You need a jacket. Here." She handed me her jean jacket and I pulled it on. It smelled like the perfume she'd started wearing. She pulled a wool sweater over her head and we started quickly down the hill toward the beach together.

I didn't waste any time. I didn't think I had much.

"Look, I know I've been acting strange. I know you probably don't think of me as a sane person right now but I need you to know some things about Fin."

"Like what?"

We crossed the highway and I looked around quickly for any sign of Fin's truck.

"I think Fin killed Lucky. I do. I know that sounds nuts to you but hear me out."

"No! Stop it, George! You've got to stop this."

We were standing in the sand now, facing each other. I took her hands in mine. "I don't have time to tell you everything right now, but I will, I promise. The important thing is that you know that he's dangerous."

She shook her head and yanked her hands out of

mine. "Goddamnit, George! You ruin everything, you know that? No wonder Lucky was always traveling. You drove him crazy."

"No, no, no." I was starting to babble. "This is different, just listen."

"No. I won't. You listen to me. I'm pregnant."

I stared at her. Even though I'd known for weeks, to hear her say it was like a punch in the stomach.

"Georgia, I'm having a baby. I mean *we* are."

Tears appeared, streaming down my cheeks.

"Fin wants us to have a life together right here in False Bay."

I looked away. My eyes traveled far down the beach to where Rocket was chasing seagulls. I remembered that first day we ran into Fin on the beach. Fin had robbed me of everything good in my life. I couldn't think of anything except how Lucky would feel about this, how devastated he would be.

"And there's more . . ." she said.

I braced myself.

"We're getting married." She put her hands on my shoulders like she was physically trying to stop me from reacting the way she probably knew I would.

"Married?"

"Yes! Be happy for me, please be happy for me."

I couldn't be happy for her. This meant that Fin was all the way in now. No one could doubt him now that he was about to start a family. How absolutely perfect, the girlfriend of False Bay's favorite son. He couldn't have devised it any better.

"He's dangerous, Sonia." I could feel myself getting wound up. I wanted to stop but I couldn't. I was afraid for her. I was afraid for me too. "My brother dies and suddenly this guy who obviously loves you magically turns up like there's a job opening and he's *just* the guy to fill it and nothing about that strikes you as odd? I know things about him that you don't know. He came to the hospital. He threatened me!"

"I'm leaving." She trudged up the beach. I ran behind her and yanked her back. Her eyes burned. She grabbed me by my shoulders and looked directly into my eyes. "Georgia, you *have* to stop this, okay? I get it. Things have been tough for you around here but please, just stop. I know Fin. I love him."

I looked down at my feet. She dropped her arms to her sides and I looked up. Her eyes were closed.

"You're still hanging on to Lucky so tight. You have to let him go." She opened her eyes.

"I can't," I said.

"I think he'd want me to be happy. Don't you?"

"Next time I see him I'll be sure to ask him." I turned abruptly and started walking briskly away from her.

"George!" she called my name again and again. I kept walking, up the beach away from her. I wanted to be far away from her. Rocket ran alongside me, looking up at me, confused.

It wasn't Sonia's fault Fin showed up in False Bay, but maybe just this once I was right about something. I wasn't crazy. Fin wanted all of this. He wanted everything Lucky had. He wanted it enough to kill him.

I had to find proof, though, and I had to find it fast or no one would ever believe me.

TWENTY EIGHT

"Honey, I think it's time to wash that T-shirt," said my mom. She sat across from me at the kitchen table with a mug of tea.

I looked down at Lucky's shirt. It was white once but now it was a dull gray. Bugs Bunny had a smear of something brown across his ears. Still, I couldn't take it off. My headaches were all gone, but now there were whisperings in my head. Sometimes they were louder than other times but they specifically told me that the shirt stays on. I tapped away on my laptop. I tapped the floor with my foot.

"What are you working on there?" asked my mom.

"Nothing."

"Your fingers are moving awfully fast for someone who's doing nothing."

"Mom, please."

I stood up with my laptop still open.

"Where are you going?" asked my mom. "Your dad and I want to talk to you about . . ."

"No!" I said. "No hospitals." I could feel her worry as she watched me walk away.

I went into my bedroom and closed the door. I was running out of time. I needed to get real proof that Fin killed my brother, and I couldn't do it with someone staring at me with a furrowed brow. Ever since I'd spoken to Professor Hastings that day, I'd been wondering about Kelly Hastings, his brother. He'd said that Kelly and Fin went to Julliard together. I kept wondering about what had happened to Kelly. Why hadn't Professor Hastings offered me his brother's phone number if they were friends? I'd tried a few searches online, but I hadn't been able to find the right Kelly Hastings. Suddenly, an idea occurred to me. I typed in his name again, and "New York" and "obituary." There it was. My pulse quickened.

Kelly Hastings was dead.

The obituary said that he had died in a rock climbing accident four years earlier. He was survived by his loving family: His father, Winston Hastings (founder of the Hastings Foundation, a nonprofit organization whose mission it is to award college scholarships to underprivileged children or children from foster families); his mother, Mavis Hastings, who was head of the board of trustees for Carnegie Hall; and his brother, Sam Hastings, a professor at NYU. I was sure now that Kelly Hastings was the boy in the photos I'd found in the redwood cottage: the one on the boat and the one in the candid photos. There had been another "accident," and another friend of Fin's was dead. A coincidence? No way.

I lay there on my bed, pondering all of this. It was becoming harder and harder to concentrate, but I forced myself to focus. I clicked on the icon for the video Jesse had sent me. I kept it on my desktop but I hadn't looked at it in a few weeks. Suddenly Lucky was alive on my screen. Tears welled up instantly. I watched him laughing. I missed him so much. The void he left was bad enough, but it was worse that I felt powerless to stop what was happening around me. Lucky was counting on me and I was failing miserably.

Something in the video caught my eye, and I paused on an image of Lucky. There it was, there was no mistaking it: Lucky was wearing the necklace with the fearlessness charm. I pressed "play" again. Lucky and all of his friends, including Fin, grabbed their boards and jogged to the water's edge. Jesse followed them with the camera. Just as Lucky stepped into the water, I paused it again. Lucky was still wearing the necklace. Fin told me that Lucky gave him that necklace, but that wasn't possible. Lucky died that day. A tear rolled down my cheek. Had Fin taken the necklace, from my brother's neck after he was dead, or did he do it while he was drowning him? I pulled the necklace out of the front pocket of my jeans and hooked the silver clasp around my neck. I touched the charm. I had to talk to Sonia again, but I had no idea how to make her listen to me.

TWENTY NINE

A wall of exhaustion hit me. I sprawled on the sofa with the intention of shutting my eyes for a minute. I wanted to think about what to do next. I woke up hours later. I sat up and rubbed my eyes. My glasses were on the table. I put them on and looked around the room. Rocket looked up at me from where he'd been sleeping on the floor. The rest of the house was dark, and the door to my mom and dad's bedroom was closed. The TV was still on. A blond woman in a crisp red suit was reading the news. I found the remote under the pillow. I was about to click the TV off when something the newswoman was saying caught my attention.

"A young local man was found drowned off the coast of Northern California near Laurel Point this afternoon. Police are not releasing his name until the victim's family has been notified. Police are unclear as to what caused the man to drown. He's said to have been an excellent swimmer. The police are asking anyone who may have been in the area at the time to come forward. The young man was with a group of his friends on the beach this afternoon. Police have taken reports from all but one of them. They are working to locate that man. As of now he is still at large. Police are saying that foul play has not been ruled out in the victim's drowning."

I stared at the TV. The TV newswoman was looking directly at me. She was talking to me. She was sending me a message. It was important that I didn't screw it up. Not this time.

I had to figure out what to do. I had to figure out whom to tell. I had to do it soon, or more people would die.

"I won't screw it up this time," I said to the newswoman.

Fine. I'd been mistaken about the drifter at Ralph's gas station, but there had been another time, when I was in fifth grade, that things could have turned out differently. I became obsessed with a girl in my grade named Portia. She and I lived in completely different worlds. She was a junior beauty queen and perfectly suited for pageant life. Her long black hair was always brushed to a sheen and held back with pretty hair bands. I was already "the weird kid," all legs and teeth. I wore thick glasses and I dressed like a boy. I used to stand by my locker and watch Portia float down the school hallway with an entourage of girls who were pale imitations of her.

At the beginning of sixth grade, I arrived at school to the news that Portia had vanished from her house the night before. The entire school was buzzing. Search parties were organized, flyers were posted everywhere, volunteers sprang into action. I became completely preoccupied with the missing girl and I watched all the interviews on the TV news. Portia's parents were divorced. Portia's mom, a former beauty queen herself who ran a nail salon, dramatically implored the kidnapper to "bring her baby back safe." Portia's dad, who was now remarried and living in North Carolina, came back and headed up the command center. I watched him closely on TV. He had a way of looking away whenever he mentioned his daughter's name. I told my mom that I thought Portia's dad was hiding something. She wouldn't take me seriously.

The story eventually died down and people stopped talking about it, but I kept thinking about Portia and where she could be.

A few years later, a woman in North Carolina saw a teenage girl buying nails and screws at a hardware store. The girl looked like the artist's rendering of the now fourteen-year-old Portia she'd seen on a TV show called *Missing Persons,* except her long black hair had been cut short. The woman called the cops, and a SWAT team surrounded Portia's dad's house, which was two blocks from the hardware store. They found Portia in the basement. She'd been drugged, brainwashed, and held prisoner by her wingnut dad and his crazy wife. Portia was back on the TV news, looking pale and haunted as she quietly described her horrible existence. While Portia was gone, her mom had married a cop from the case and they'd had a baby girl together. The new family looked really uncomfortable together on TV.

"I could have saved her," I said to the TV newswoman.

My dad opened the bedroom door.

"Hi, Dad."

"It's late," he said

I looked over at the clock. It was three a.m.

"Sorry."

"Who were you talking to?"

"No one."

"Please, George, just go to bed."

THIRTY

I pulled my clothes off and got into bed. I finally fell asleep, but my eyes flew open again just as the sky was growing light. I got up and pulled on some sweats and Lucky's Bugs Bunny T-shirt and left the house quickly. My dad would be up soon. I knew that if I hung around, he and my mom would definitely put me in the hospital. I trotted down the hill toward the Heron to hide out and do some baking, at least till my mom went into her studio to work. I needed some time to figure out what to do next.

I smelled bacon when I came in the back door of the Inn. Karl looked up from the grill when he heard me come in.

"Hey." He looked around quickly. "Look, I shouldn't

be telling you this but Jeff and Miles are mega-pissed at you."

"Yeah? Why?"

I walked into the pantry and grabbed my apron and my clogs.

"You don't even know?"

"No, I don't even know. Tell me."

"The muffins, man. You didn't do the muffins."

How could I have forgotten to bake the muffins?

"Oh, shit, right."

Why was he looking at me like that? What did he know?

"Plus, they ran out of dessert like two days ago. Guess you didn't leave enough in the walk-in. Marc had to whip up a bunch of crème brûlée, so he wants you dead. You look like shit, by the way, maybe worse than shit."

"Shut up." Coming here was a bad idea.

Karl shrugged and went back to work.

The swinging door flew open and Jeff appeared, carrying a coffee mug. It was too late to run.

"Georgia," he said crisply. "Finally. Thank you for stopping by."

"Sorry, I guess I lost track of my days." How many days had it been?

"You lost track of your days? How does that

happen?" He wrinkled up his nose. "Have you showered lately?"

No. I had not.

"Look, if you're going to fire me, fire away."

"Didn't you get my phone messages? I must have left about ten."

"I lost my phone." As I was saying that I realized that it was true. I hadn't seen my phone in days. Had someone stolen it? Who? Fin?

"As I've said before, I'm really sorry about Lucky, and I'm sure it's all been very hard on you, but we need someone making desserts that we can count on, and, well, lately, you seem a bit . . ."

Just then Fin strolled into the kitchen like he'd been standing outside, waiting for just the right moment. He looked at me and then at Jeff and Karl. "I'm sensing some tension in this kitchen."

I spun around to face him. I reared up and unleashed all of my pent-up anxiety and frustration on him. "How did you kill Kelly Hastings?" I shouted.

Fin's eyes flickered but he composed himself. "Who?" he asked.

"You know who. Did you get him to trust you first, just like Lucky trusted you?"

Jeff and Karl looked from Fin to me and back to Fin.

"My brother told me everything. He showed me how you killed him. I know what you did. I already told Sonia too."

"George, I think maybe we need to get you out of here," Fin said. "Why don't you let me drive you home?" He lunged toward me.

I grabbed a knife out of the knife block on the prep table and waved it at him. "Stay away from me," I shouted. He took a step back.

Jeff and Karl took a step back too. "Georgia," said Jeff. "Please put the knife down. Get your things and get out of here, or I'll call the police."

"Fine!" I let the knife clatter to the floor. I balled up my apron and hurled it into the pantry.

"And you know what?" I spat. "I don't need this job. I'm too busy for this shit. Things are going down around here that no one sees but me. Things like *that* guy," I pointed at Fin, "is a murderer. He killed my brother."

Fin looked amused but he didn't move.

"And I'm the only one around here who seems to care while the rest of you blow smoke up his ass. And keeping track of it all? That is a full-time job! I don't have time for things like . . . like baking fucking cupcakes."

"Muffins," said Jeff quietly.

Karl snorted.

"Shut up, Karl!" I said, looking menacingly at him. He took another step back. I grabbed my backpack and got out of there.

I walked quickly south, up the side of the highway, away from the Inn, away from False Bay. I looked over my shoulder every few seconds. I took deep breaths. I tried to calm down. I had to get off the main road. I turned off the highway onto a road lined with redwoods that took me inland. The road looked familiar but I wasn't sure I knew it. I needed to find a place to rest and get something to drink. I was so thirsty and so tired. I needed to map out a plan. I had to get organized. If I went home, my mom would take me to the hospital. I couldn't go there. I had no job, nowhere to go, nothing to do, no one who loved me. I longed to talk to Lucky. He would know what to do. He always did. One thing I knew for sure, though: Fin would come for me and it would be soon. I had to go underground.

My feet were getting heavy, but I kept walking. About a half mile up the road I came to a campground I recognized. It was the same campground where Lucky's friends had stayed when we had the party. I walked quickly along the perimeter, not wanting to be seen. There were a few tents set up at campsites. A couple of campers were cooking breakfast on fire pits and the smell of woodsmoke filled the air. I kept walking till I found an unoccupied campsite away from the campers. I took my backpack off and sat down at a wooden picnic table. The sun streamed through the redwoods. There was a water spigot not far away. I got up stiffly and walked over to it, turned it on, and cupped my hands under the cool running water to splash it onto my face. Then I kneeled under the spigot and drank.

Back at the picnic table I looked through my backpack. There wasn't much in there. I had my wallet but there was only three dollars in it. I had a half a pack of gum, Lucky's book, his Swiss Army Knife, a Bic lighter, and a pen. I tried to think of what to do next. It was getting harder and harder to focus. My brain played tricks on me, feeding me a thought that seemed to make sense for a second and then confusing me by pelting me with hundreds of thoughts, so many that I couldn't sort through them, I couldn't choose.

On the inside back cover of the book, I wrote down a list of things I needed to do:

1. Find someone I can trust—*Sharona*? If something happens to me, someone else needs to know the truth.

2. Get something to defend myself with, a weapon—*A gun? From where?*
3. Plan an escape route—If I kept traveling inland, maybe I could hitch a ride.
4. Get some money out of the bank—*How? Use my Culinary Institute fund?*
5. Get shelter somewhere safe, just for now—*Where?*

"You mind if I sit down?"

I spun around. An old guy wearing camouflage pants, hiking boots, and a backpack was approaching. He carried a gnarled walking stick.

"Easy there. Didn't mean to scare ya."

I looked around the campground. There were lots of empty picnic tables.

"I wouldn't mind a little company," he said. Had he read my mind?

"Uh, sure, okay."

"Whatcha got there?" he said, picking up my book as he sat down. "Vonnegut?"

"It's actually not mine. Please put it down."

He set it down. "Vonnegut's good. That's not his best but it's not bad. You want some beef jerky?"

"No, thanks."

He pulled out a small ziplock plastic bag and

popped a piece in his mouth. "Nice day. You live around here?"

"Why do you want to know where I live?"

"Just making conversation. I live in Petaluma. I'm just passing through here. I found some nice trails up there through the redwoods." He pointed.

"Are you alone?" I looked around quickly.

"Yes."

"Who do you work for?"

"I work for myself. I'm a doctor, semiretired. I like to get out on my days off. My wife passed away a few years ago and I bought a backpack and I just started walking. Now I can't seem to stop." He chuckled.

That sounded like something he said a lot. Maybe it was something he said so that people wouldn't feel sorry for him, a lonely old widower, walking through the woods by himself. Or maybe it was all a lie. Maybe Dr. Saul had sent him.

"Do you know Dr. Saul?" I narrowed my eyes.

"Dr. Saul? No, I don't think so. What kind of doctor is he?"

"A shrink."

He looked at me differently now. "I'm a pediatrician."

I looked up through the trees. Something blue dangling from a tree branch caught my eye. I realized that it was a blue flipper. This was the oak tree where

Lucky's friends had hung all the mementos. The doctor looked over at the tree.

"What is that?"

"A flipper."

"A flipper? Are you sure? What would a flipper be doing hanging from a coast live oak tree?"

He seemed like the kind of guy who took pride in always getting the names of things correct, a smarty-pants.

"My brother died surfing. His friends hung a bunch of stuff in that tree, stuff to remember him by."

"I'm very sorry. When did he die?"

I shook my head vigorously. I didn't like what was happening. "I don't remember."

He looked at me closely. "Hey, are you feeling okay?"

"Not really."

"Where are your parents?"

"I don't know."

"Are they at home?"

"My parents are working. They work. Why all the questions?"

"Do they know you're here? Can I call them for you? Do you need help?"

"No, no, and no."

It occurred to me suddenly that it was kind of

odd how he came up to me like that, out of nowhere, all casual and wanting to sit with me. Maybe he even followed me here. Maybe he worked for Fin. My scalp went all prickly. Maybe word was out that I was trying to go underground.

"You know, I think I *will* call my mom. Can I borrow your cell phone for a minute?"

"Yeah, sure." He unzipped the pocket of his back-pack and handed me his phone.

"Thanks." I grabbed my pack and started walking away from the picnic table.

"Hey, where are you going?"

I started walking faster.

"Georgia!"

How did he know my name? I hadn't told him my name.

I started running.

THIRTY ONE

I heard the old man calling for me, but once I was away from the campground and inside the forest I was pretty sure he wouldn't find me. I dropped my backpack and sat next to it on a carpet of leaves and pine needles. I hugged my knees. I put the phone down next to me. I knew I had to get rid of it. Cell phones can be traced. I picked it up and clicked through the recent calls. There was nothing I recognized. I dialed Sonia's number. The phone rang a few times. I was ready to hang up and then she picked up.

"Hello?"

I couldn't speak.

"George, is that you? Talk to me. I'm so worried about you."

She waited. "I can hear you breathing, George. I

heard about what happened at the Inn. Please talk to me. I'm sorry about before."

I clicked the phone off. Fin had already gotten to Sonia. It was too late to intercept the bullshit he probably told her about me.

I wanted to carry on but my legs couldn't move anymore. I would rest here for a few minutes and then ditch the phone. I didn't have a jacket or a sweater with me but it was warm for now. I curled up on the ground and used my backpack as a pillow. Just a few minutes, I told myself.

When I woke up the temperature had dipped and I was shivering. My bare ankles were covered in insect bites, my face too. I could feel my right eye swelling up. The sun was low in the sky. I heard a helicopter. I looked up through the tops of the redwoods. The helicopter was hovering directly above the small stand of trees I was hiding in. The phone. It had to be the phone. I waited until the helicopter moved off a bit and then I grabbed my pack and wound my way down through the scrub manzanita and the tall grasses, keeping low to the ground. Below me I saw a pullout and staging area for a walking trail down to a beach. There was a public bathroom there, but I would have to cross the highway. The helicopter was louder now. I crashed down to the road and darted across two lanes like a small animal. I made a beeline for the bathroom and dropped the phone into the inground toilet. I looked up at the sky. The helicopter was still a ways off, but it had turned around now and it was headed back toward me. The *thwap-thwap-thwap* sound that the blades made was deafening. I dashed back across the highway and scrambled up the rocky embankment that ran along the road. I dove into the brush. I decided to wait there till I felt safer. "Please go away," I said, over and over, as I rocked back and forth.

When it started to get dark I headed back inland. I was cold now and exhausted and I wanted to go home, but I couldn't go there. Especially not the way I looked now. I wished Lucky were here to help me. Maybe he didn't know how to find me out here. What if that were true? I could build a fire. That's what I would do. Like when we were kids, a signal fire. I made my way back to the campground. A few more people had set up tents. Lanterns were lit and fires burned at each campsite. People sat around their fires in lawn chairs, talking and laughing. I walked quickly past them unseen. I walked all the way to the far end of the campground where there was no one. I put my backpack down next to the fire pit and walked over to a cinderblock open-ended shed filled with firewood. I hauled a few pieces and some kindling back to the site and dropped them in the fire pit. I took the lighter out of my pack and built a pile of dry leaves, pine needles, and grass under the kindling. I clicked the lighter several times. My fingers were numb and shaking. I finally got it to catch and a tiny flame appeared. I added more and more kindling and then a small piece of wood. I blew gently on it till it caught. I added a couple of bigger pieces. I finally had a real fire.

I lay down next to the fire with my head on my backpack and looked up at the stars while I waited for Lucky. I put my hands between my thighs and fell asleep. I dreamt that there were hundreds of helicopters like giant flying bugs chasing me through an open field. I ran till I dropped from exhaustion. I covered the back of my head with my hands and waited for them to carry me away.

I woke suddenly to a sharp stabbing pain in my spine. I opened my left eye. My right eye wouldn't open. It was daylight. My fire was out, and I was numb and stiff with cold. I felt around till I found my glasses on the ground next to me and put them on. I rolled over and sat up quickly. Two kids, a boy and a girl, were standing over me. They looked startled. The boy held a sharpened stick with burnt marshmallow goo on the end. They took a quick step back.

"What the hell?" My voice came out strained and husky.

"We thought you were dead," said the boy.

"Get out of here!"

They darted back to their campsite, a few camp-sites away, shouting, "Mom!"

Their mom appeared and they said something to her, pointing at me. She gathered them to her and watched me. Her husband joined her with his hands on his hips.

"Hey! What is your fucking problem?" I shouted at them. "I have as much right to be here as you do!"

I saw the husband take out his cell and punch some numbers.

"I didn't do anything!" I shouted. I grabbed my pack and ran deeper into the campground till I was out of sight. I came to another water spigot. I couldn't remember the last time I ate or drank. I felt like a shadow. I looked at my hands. They were black. My fingernails were ragged and filthy. I could smell my own sweat. I could smell my own fear. I washed my hands and gulped some water. I put my pack on and started walking. I stopped several times to check the sky for helicopters. It was clear for now but it was hard to hear them coming above the now constant chatter in my head: *Don't trust anyone. I can hear you breathing. Is he dangerous? Please be happy for me. Are you okay? I'm pregnant. You passed out. I'm recommending hospitalization. We're going to have to let you go . . .*

I made it back down to the highway. I stopped next to the road and stayed crouched in the underbrush to see if the coast was clear before carrying on. I saw Fin's truck coming up the road toward me, moving slow. He was scanning both sides of the highway, looking for me. My heart pounded in my chest. I stayed there, perfectly still, till he was out of sight. Then I walked down to the shoulder. I was moving as fast as I could, but a sharp pain shot up my right leg whenever I took a step. I'd walked for at least a mile when I heard honking behind me. I started jogging as fast as I could, but that wasn't very fast. I heard a car door slam. I heard someone calling my name. I felt a hand on my shoulder.

"George, didn't you hear me?"

I spun around. It was Sharona. Her eyes grew wide when she saw me.

"Oh my God." She took a step back. "What in the hell happened to you?"

I lowered my eyes. I was ashamed. "Nothing. I went camping. That's all."

"Here, get in my car."

"I can't go home."

"No, no. I promise I won't take you home. Just get in my car and talk to me for a minute, okay?"

She held my elbow as I limped back to where her car was pulled crookedly off the highway and got in. Sharona got in the driver's side. She dug through the backseat and came up with a hooded sweatshirt.

"Here. Put this on. You're shivering."

I pulled the sweatshirt over my head.

"Okay, what's going on? Who did this to you? Did someone hurt you?"

I shook my head.

"Then what? What happened to your eye?"

I exhaled. "You wouldn't understand."

"Try me."

"People are following me."

"What people?"

I pointed to the sky.

"God?"

"No."

"Come to my house with me. My mom's at work. I'll protect you," she said naively, like she could.

"I can't. I'm waiting for Lucky to contact me again. And if Fin finds me he'll kill me. He wants me dead."

"Fin? What do you mean?"

"Lucky talks to me. He wants me to help him."

"Help him what?"

I stared out the windshield.

"George, help him what?" She raised her voice in frustration.

"Stop him."

"Stop who?"

"Fin. Fin killed Lucky. Lucky wants me to stop him before he kills someone else."

Sharona looked out the windshield and shook her head. "Okay, look, I'm going to take you to my house, okay? You'll be safe there."

"I can't. I have to get out of here." I grabbed for the door handle.

"Wait! Please! Come to my house and we'll sort everything out there."

I looked at her. I wanted to trust her.

"Please."

I let go of the door handle.

Sharona pulled back onto the road. She started driving north. I hunkered down in the seat and pulled the hood of the sweatshirt over my head.

The house was small but tidy and bright. Sharona took me by the hand and led me to the bathroom.

"Get undressed. I think you should wash your hair. Can you do that?"

I shrugged.

"You get in the shower and I'm going to make you some tea. Are you hungry?"

"I think so."

"I'll make you some soup." She closed the door.

I pulled off my clothes. They smelled really bad so I wrapped everything in a towel except Lucky's Bugs Bunny T-shirt. In Sharona's bright bathroom mirror I looked like a ghoul. My hair hung in long, greasy strands. My right eye was completely closed and I had swollen bites up and down my arms and on my neck. I was filthy. Sharona poked her head in the door. I quickly covered my naked body with a towel but I saw the shock in her eyes when she saw my rib cage and my bony hips. "Here, I brought you a pair of my jeans and a T-shirt. They're too big for you but they're clean," she said.

I didn't want to get in the shower. I wasn't sure I could trust Sharona; I was afraid that she would call someone. But I turned the water on and got in quickly while it was still cold. I scrubbed myself as fast as I could. My hair was so tangled that I couldn't even get my fingers through it. I turned the shower off and stepped out. In the medicine cabinet, I found a small pair of scissors and started cutting. Damp coils of blond hair fell onto my bare feet. I hacked away, closer and closer to my scalp, until my hair was short and jagged. I put my glasses back on and was startled at what I saw. I didn't know who I was looking at.

I heard Sharona talking on the phone. I quietly cracked the bathroom door and listened.

". . . I found her limping up the highway, looking half dead." There was a pause. I pulled on my underwear, the Bugs Bunny T-shirt, and Sharona's clothes.

"I can't put her on. She's showering. No, don't come over here. I promised her I wouldn't call anyone."

I grabbed my backpack.

"Okay, I'll try and get her in the car. Honestly, though, I think she needs a hospital."

"Go!" said the voices. They said it loud. I tiptoed down the small hallway, grabbed my sneakers, and pushed the screen door open. The spring made a whining sound. I leapt off the porch and ran through Sharona's neighbor's backyard. I heard the door whine open again. Sharona was on the porch now. She called out to me but I kept running. I headed toward a hedge on the far side of the next property. I crouched down, panting like a wild animal. I sat there like that for a minute till Sharona stopped calling my name. Maybe she was going for help. I picked the pebbles out of the soles of my feet and quickly pulled my sneakers on. I heard voices coming from the trees above my head. I clapped my hands over my ears but I could still hear them. They bled into the breeze in the treetops and the ocean below. They sounded like a hundred whispering children.

Sharona or someone else, someone worse, would come looking for me soon. I waited a few minutes, and then I crossed the highway and headed inland and over the hill in the direction of my house to come at it from behind. I remembered an old equipment shed at the top of the hill behind our house. It sat at the back of a small pasture on the bluff. Lucky knew about it. We used to play there when we were kids. He could find me there. I prayed it was still standing. I found the path and started moving faster. The path would take me just north of Sonia's house but it would be a long walk, especially with my injured right leg. Sharona's jeans slid off my hips every few steps but I yanked them up and kept moving. I could watch for Fin's truck on the highway from the path. I checked the sky for the helicopters again. Nothing yet, but they would show up soon. A police cruiser appeared, traveling slowly north on the highway. I froze until he was well past me. After about an hour I came up next to Sonia's house. There were no cars in the driveway. I walked quickly past her kitchen window and started up the hill past my own house. Fin's red truck was in the driveway next to my mom's Volvo. My dad's truck wasn't there. I crept along the fence line and quietly opened the gate and then darted through it and hid behind the jasmine where I could see into my mom's studio. My mom was in there, sitting with her back to me at her worktable with her head in her hands. Fin was sitting next to her, his arm wrapped around her shoulders.

I couldn't remember when I'd last been home. Was it yesterday? My brain didn't offer me the information. Maybe it had been longer. Maybe they thought I was dead. But Sharona had called them. When was that?

I caught a glimpse of my reflection in the glass window. With my glasses and my swollen eye and my hair hacked off I could be mistaken for homeless, yet I was standing five feet from my home. Fin lifted his head and slowly turned toward the window. I froze. He sensed me. His eyes came to rest on me. I stumbled back through the gate and started along the path that led up the hill above our house.

THIRTY TWO

I stopped several times on the path up to the shed. There was a terrible pressure on my lungs. Every breath I took was painful and my temples pounded. I felt feverish and clammy, and then I felt so cold that my teeth chattered. I stumbled and fell down once, tearing Sharona's jeans and scraping my knee. A trickle of blood started down my leg. I contemplated staying there on the ground like that but then I slowly, painfully, got myself back up and carried on. When I finally arrived at the top I was so light-headed I felt I might pass out. I stood there for a moment, trying to catch my breath. My nose had started to bleed, and I wiped at it. An angry smudge of blood appeared on my forearm. I looked down at my house. Fin's truck wasn't parked next to my mom's in the driveway anymore. I continued up a path that led through some trees and then into the old pasture.

The dilapidated equipment shed was still there. I walked as quickly as I could toward it and staggered through the wide doorway. Hundreds of pigeons were perched high in the rafters. Except for a couple of empty beer cans in the corner, it looked abandoned. I dropped my backpack and fell to the dirt floor. I lay on my back, looking up at the sky through the missing boards on the roof. My head was spinning. Would Lucky remember this place? I would wait here for him. My eyes started to close and I was sure that I would die in this spot. I fought to stay conscious. I wanted to be awake if Lucky was coming. This was a good place to wait for him. Maybe he could tell me what to do next. I drifted off for a bit. I don't know how long. When I opened my eyes, the voices started again, whispering at first and then mumbling something. The voices were coming from the pigeons above me. I tried to understand what they were saying, but I could only make out some of the words: *Dead, water, black, water, neck? Fire, Fire, Fire!* They watched me with their beady red eyes.

I smelled woodsmoke. Something near me was burning. I lifted my head painfully. After a moment I saw it. One tiny flame curling lazily up the walls of the shed. A few more danced along the ground, then a few more. Then flames leapt angrily up all four walls. The pigeons flapped their wings and took off in a flock, rushing the door. I watched the fire take over. I heard a loud creak and a piece of a rafter, alive with flames, came crashing down, landing inches from my feet. I dug my heels in and pushed myself back as another piece fell. I raised my hands to protect myself and tried to stand but the wood knocked me back down to the dirt floor. I started to cough. The smoke was black and thick now. I struggled to get up but I had nothing left. Someone was moving along the side of the shed, coming toward me, through the flames. Fin.

I dragged myself pathetically away from him.

"Where ya going?" he stood on my hand with his boot. I screamed out in pain.

"You're such a confounding girl, George. And I've got to hand it to you, you don't give up so easy."

I grimaced in pain.

"Aaah, there's the face. You know, Lucky had exactly the same series of expressions on his face when I held him under: confusion, and then panic, followed by understanding, and finally, acceptance. He fought hard too, but in the end he went quietly, one bubble at a time, smaller and smaller and then . . . well . . . you know the rest, don't you?"

The flames were approaching him from behind. I tried to move again but I couldn't.

"You won't get away with this," I croaked.

"I've already gotten away with it. When are you going to get it? I'm not leaving. You are. I've worked hard for what I have now. Not like Lucky. Everything came to him so damn easy that he took it all for granted. Not anymore."

"Please . . . don't."

"It's your doing, George. If you would have shut the hell up, we could have all been so happy together. Couldn't you have just played along? You ruined everything. And there's nothing you could have done that would bring Lucky back. And now you've thrown away your own life too. What a waste." He shook his head.

There was another loud crack. Another rafter beam fell, hitting Fin on the right shoulder. He fell to the ground, disappearing into the thick black smoke. Then, from behind me I felt arms gathering me up. I was off the ground now. I was moving. I saw the taut tendons in Lucky's neck as he strained to carry me out of there to safety. I coughed and gasped for breath.

"Wait here," he said. "I'll be right back." But it wasn't his voice. It was Sonia's. I heard footsteps running away from me. Everything went dark.

I woke up on the ground outside the shed, coughing. My lungs burned. I held my hands out in front of my face. Blisters were starting to appear on my palms. My skin curled up like tissue paper. Over my shoulder, the shed blazed. I looked around for Fin, but I couldn't see him. I called out for Lucky. My voice was a dry rasp. I curled up in the dirt, coughing, and squeezed my eyes shut. I would stay here like this, listening to sirens off in the distance, until Lucky came back. I hoped it would be soon.

A few moments later there were loud voices everywhere, but someone was right next to me, speaking quietly to me and touching me carefully. I was lifted onto a stretcher. I turned my head and I saw a police car and a policeman. I saw the back of Fin. He was handcuffed and he was being led, limping, to the police car. Sonia was talking to another policeman. She was pointing at the shed and then at Fin and then at me. She was crying. They put Fin in the back of the car and shut the door. He watched me out the window as the car drove away.

THIRTY THREE

I remember hearing voices around my head, saying things I didn't understand, and the sound of a siren and the feeling of speed, but I kept my eyes squeezed shut. Much later my eyes fluttered open in a small room. The walls were painted swimming-pool turquoise. I felt a peaceful floating-on-water feeling, like when you go to a public aquarium and you stand in those darkened rooms and watch the fish glide by slowly on the other side of the glass. Bubbles and ripples of light reflected onto the walls. My head was quiet. The voices seemed to be gone. My wrists were tethered to the bed with restraints. My right hand was heavily bandaged and my left hand had bandages around a couple of fingers. I felt drugged. I lifted my head with effort and looked around. Lucky dozed in a plastic chair next to my bed.

"Lucky," I whispered.

His eyes opened and he smiled. "There you are, George. I was so worried."

"Am I dead?"

"'Course not."

"What happened?"

"You fell down a hole."

"I did?"

"Yes. But you're back now." He stood up and bent over to kiss the top of my head.

"Where're my glasses?" I asked.

"What glasses? You don't wear glasses."

I looked down at my hair. It lay in long strands against my hospital gown. It looked silky and smooth and fell around me like I was Sleeping Beauty.

"My hair," I said.

"It was all tangled so I brushed it. You want to see?"

"Yes."

He produced a hand mirror and held it up to my face. "See? Beautiful."

I smiled. I did look beautiful. My face was full and round and my eyes were bright. I was back to my old self—I was *better* than my old self.

"Why are my hands tied up?"

"Because you bit me," he said, but he wasn't Lucky anymore; he was a dark-skinned man in a white doctor's jacket.

I tried to focus my eyes to look around. The room was beige in every way. A bag hung on a metal thing with a tube that was attached to my hand with tape. The man in the jacket smiled warmly. "Welcome back, Georgia. How do you feel?" He had an English accent.

"Who are you?"

"I'm Richard. You're at UCSF. I'm an intern here. We're going to help you get well."

"Where's Lucky?"

"Is Lucky your dog?"

"No, he's my brother."

"Well, maybe he's waiting outside with your parents."

"Maybe."

"I'll take the restraints off if you promise to behave."

"Okay."

He unbuckled one and then the other.

"There you are. Free as a bird."

I felt my hair. It was cut close to my scalp. It felt ragged and horrible. There were painful raised pink welts on my arms. I touched my right eye. It was still swollen shut.

"Poison oak," said Richard.

A tear rolled down my cheek.

Richard grabbed a tissue and touched it to my cheek. "Aw, hey, don't do that. You're going to be okay. I promise."

"Do you know where my glasses are?"

"I do, actually." He pulled open a drawer next to my bed and handed them to me. "I want you to get some rest. We're going to get you hydrated and get you eating again and you'll feel a lot better, okay?"

I nodded. I wanted him to leave. I wanted to cry in peace.

"I'll send your mom and dad in."

I remembered something important. "Hey, Richard?"

"Yes?"

"Did you see my T-shirt? I need my T-shirt."

He opened the little door on my bedside table and pulled out a plastic bag. He showed me the filthy, tattered Bugs Bunny T-shirt. It was cut open, right down the middle.

"Sorry. Looks like it didn't make it. We were trying to get you hooked up quickly. Maybe your parents can get you a new one? Or maybe your brother?"

"Thanks," I said.

"Not too long. She's been sedated," I heard him tell my parents as he passed them in the doorway. I put my glasses on.

My mom started to cry when she saw me. She awkwardly tried to hug me without hurting me. My dad put his hand gently on my arm. My eyes were too heavy. I couldn't keep them open. I slipped into a deep sleep.

THIRTY FOUR

Over the next few days I drifted in and out of consciousness. I started to feel better. Whatever meds they gave me seemed to be working. I did a lot of sleeping and the committee in my brain diminished and then disappeared. It was like I'd been listening to speed metal at full volume on my stereo and then someone suddenly yanked the cord out of the wall. I hadn't realized just how loud they'd become. It felt luxurious to just lie there and think one thought at a time, one *logical* thought at a time.

My mom brought me some new clothes and gave me a haircut. A sort of terrible pixie was the best she could do with the hack job I'd done in Sharona's bathroom. I felt it with my one good hand, but I put a towel over the mirror in the bathroom so I wouldn't see what I looked like. The welts on my arms and legs were disappearing, and soon my eye opened up again.

My mom sat by my bed one afternoon. "George, I have to talk to you about something," she said.

"Okay."

"When we lost Lucky, it was the end of the world for me. I didn't know how I was going to go on. I lost myself in my grief."

She stroked my choppy hair.

"But when I saw you lying on the ground outside that shed, burned and bleeding and wasted away to nothing"—tears started to spill down her cheeks—"I thought you were dead and I felt like dying myself because I finally realized that all this time I never really understood how much you were suffering. I was so impatient with you." She put her head in my lap. "I'm so sorry. Please forgive me. I can't imagine how much pain you must have been in."

I patted her head gently with my bandaged hand. "It's okay, Mom."

She lifted her head. "No, it's not, it's really not. I love you, Georgia."

"I know. I love you too."

She grabbed a tissue from the box next to the bed and dabbed her eyes.

"But things will be different now. We're going to get you well." She kissed my cheek. "Okay?"

"Okay. Hey, Mom?"

"Yes?"

"You don't think Lucky kept leaving because of me, do you?"

"No, Honey. Lucky loved you very much."

"I was awful."

She smiled. "He didn't care."

The next day a doctor cut the bandage off my right hand. My palm was shiny and pink and swollen. The skin was tight and I had trouble opening my fingers.

"It will get better," she said, examining it carefully. "Every day it will get a little bit better." She smiled kindly at me. She had an accent and she told me she was from Argentina. "What does your necklace mean?" she asked, touching the silver charm at my neck.

"Fearlessness," I said. "It's Sanskrit."

"I like that."

I started physical therapy for my hand and daily ninety-minute sessions with Dr. Lundgren, my new psychiatrist, in his office on the sixth floor. Dr. Lundgren seemed too young and too tall to be a psychiatrist. He was nothing at all like Dr. Saul. He had big feet and hands and large thick ears that stayed pink. His hair shot comically up off his head like broom bristles. His gait was a bit Herman Munsterish. He had a picture of his daughter on his desk, next to a spider plant. I was envious of her. She looked like a nice, normal, happy girl.

"Is that your daughter?" I asked.

"Yes. Her name is Holly," he said.

"Does she have big feet too?"

He laughed. "Yes. We buy her clown shoes."

I smiled.

The sessions were difficult. Sometimes I would stop talking for minutes at a time. Dr. Lundgren didn't seem bothered by this. He was very patient.

After each session Dr. Lundgren walked me to the door. "To be continued," he'd say.

It took several sessions to tell my story. I told him about the time when I was eight and I wrapped my entire body in tinfoil and duct tape to stop the radiation from getting to my body. I also told him about the time I was ten and I dug up our dead cat, Nugget, three days after we'd buried her in the backyard because I was convinced we'd buried her alive. I told him how I stopped eating, certain I was being poisoned, and how I stopped going anywhere because I was definitely being followed, and how, when I did finally leave the house, I would have to take everything that meant anything to me with me because I thought the house wouldn't be there when I returned. It took me hours to get out of the house.

Every session was exhausting.

"Are you going to make me go back on my meds?" I asked.

"Not the same ones. We're going to try something new. I've already given you an injection. So far you seem to be responding to it very well. If it keeps working, you'll only have to get an injection once a month. I'll give you some literature on it so you'll understand it better. We'll wait and see now. We'll keep a close eye on how you're feeling."

"So, I won't see Lucky anymore," I said wistfully.

Dr. Lundgren looked at me solemnly. "Georgia, you have a mental illness. There isn't any way for you to live anything even close to a normal life without meds. You deserve a chance at happiness. Lucky would want that for you, don't you think?"

I nodded. He was right.

"We're kicking you out of here," said Dr. Lundgren at the end of our fourth session. "I'd like to keep seeing you, though, if you can manage to get to the city for appointments."

I didn't want to stop seeing him. I would have to talk to my mom and dad. I had to figure out a way to make it work.

The prospect of going back out into the real world scared me to death. I hadn't been in the hospital long, but I felt safe there.

When I left Dr. Lundgren's office that day there was a boy slouched in a chair in the waiting area. He drummed his palms against his legs. He wore a knit beanie and tinted glasses. Dyed blond hair sprouted out from underneath the hat. He looked up at me and nodded. Dr. Lundgren came out of his office.

"How are you today, Mr. Black?" he said.

The boy got up and followed Dr. Lundgren into his office.

I went to the cafeteria and loaded a tray with fish sticks and corn. I sat down at a table. I said hi to Douglas, a really nice guy who thinks he's from the future. I looked around the room. I was ready to go home.

THIRTY FIVE

Home was hard for me. I felt so vastly different from the girl who left False Bay in an ambulance. People spoke to me in simple sentences with the volume turned up as though I'd become mentally disabled and deaf somewhere along the way. I could tell by the way they kept their distance that they'd all heard the stories. My mom and dad treated me like a fragile, unstable child. They smiled way too much and watched me carefully, constantly asking me if I was hungry or tired. Even Rocket looked at me tentatively. My room was different too. They'd tidied it up and lunatic-proofed it. They took out all the matches, lighters, razors, and scissors.

Every day I felt a bit better. When I looked at myself in the mirror I still saw someone who scared me a bit, but at least I was looking in the mirror again. I had scars all over my body that only I could see. It occurred to me that I looked more like Lucky now.

I went over to Sonia's as soon as I could muster up the confidence to face her. She looked pale and drawn.

Things were awkward between us at first. She laughed nervously. "I missed you," she said.

"I wasn't gone that long."

"I think I started missing you before that. I'm so glad you're you again."

"Thank you for rescuing me. How did you know I was up there?" I asked.

"I looked out my window—you know, we were all looking for you—and I saw you on the path heading up to the bluff. You were close to the top. I was about to run after you when I saw Fin leave your mom's studio and jump in his truck. He was in a huge hurry. He was looking up at the hill. I was going to flag him down so I could go with him but he zoomed right past my house, which I found strange. I knew I could get to you pretty fast if I hiked up on the path. When I got there, the shed was already on fire. I was going to run inside, but I heard Fin talking to you, so I stayed by the door, listening." She shook her head sadly. "You tried to warn me. I should have listened. I still can't believe it."

"Yeah, me neither."

"You look so much better. I like your hair."

"Shut up."

"I do."

"How do you feel?" I gestured at her stomach.

She looked down. "I lost the baby that day you went missing."

"Oh, wow. I'm sorry."

"That's why I was a little slow getting up the path that day."

"No one told me."

"I told them not to. I wanted to tell you myself."

"Are you all right?"

"Yeah, you know . . ." she shrugged. "The doctor says I'm fine."

"What will you do?"

"I think I'll go back to school. My mom's moving in with her boyfriend, so we're giving up the house."

"You won't live here anymore?"

"I've gotta get out of this place. It's full of ghosts for me, you know?"

I did.

After I left Sonia's, I continued on down the hill. The view of the ocean as I walked was a postcard, and I wondered how long it had been since I actually saw it that way. The sun danced off the ripples on the water and the air felt crisp and clean. I felt peaceful. What a concept.

It was just a few weeks earlier but it seemed like another lifetime that I had worked at Katy's. I needed to stop by and see Sharona. She'd left several worried messages on my phone, which I'd found under my bed. I wanted to thank her for trying to help me. The bell on the door at Katy's jingled and Sharona's face lit up when she saw me. She hurried to finish ringing up a woman at the register.

"Hey stranger! I heard you were back." She hugged me tight. "Look at you! I love the short hair."

I cringed when I thought of the filthy coils of hair I'd left on her bathroom floor that horrible day.

"Oh yeah? You like it?" I ran my fingers through it and saw her look at my burned hand and quickly look away. "Hey, thanks for . . . that day . . . I was a mess."

"Don't mention it. It was pretty exciting stuff, you know, for False Bay. Wow, a psychopath, who'da thought?" She shrugged.

I still believed that the beam falling on Fin was some sort of intervention orchestrated by Lucky. I'm pretty sure Sharona would agree if I asked her, but I didn't.

"Well, I'm on my way to the Inn to ask for my job back. Wish me luck."

"You don't need it. Karl told me they're dying over there without you."

"Karl?"

"Yes, Karl. We're giving it another go."

"Seriously?"

"Yup, I guess I just can't quit that guy."

"Too bad he lasered your name off his arm."

"I know, right? Hilarious."

I remembered how I'd yelled at Karl the last time I saw him. That was another person I should apologize to.

"Hey, you can hang out at the Inn again."

"Jeff hates me."

"He does not. It's just his nature."

The bell on the door jingled again and a carload of loud tourists came in.

"I better get back to work. Katy's been working weekends with me, and oh man, is that ever brutal. I don't know how long I can hang in here."

I left Katy's and walked back up the highway to the Inn.

I took deep breaths as I opened the heavy front door. I'd composed a compelling speech, but I was nervous. I realized now that my hands needed something important to do. Creating those desserts made me happy. In the hospital I'd started thinking about the Culinary Institute again. Dr. Lundgren encouraged me to have a goal. He thought that the Institute was something I could manage easily in a year or so.

The breakfast crowd had mostly cleared out of the dining room, and Jeff and Miles were sitting together at a table when I walked in. I only had to look at their faces to know that they'd heard all the stories about me.

"Hi, Georgia," they said together with matching levels of discomfort.

"Hi."

"How are you?" said Jeff, followed by Miles who added, "Feeling?" at the end. Jeff glared at Miles.

"I'm great. Listen. I wondered if I could have my job back. I wasn't doing well when you fired me and I'm really sorry about the way I behaved but I'm much better now and I promise you can depend on me." I blurted all of it out without taking a breath.

They exchanged glances. "Oh, thank God," said Jeff. "We'd love to have you back. And we're really sorry about what happened with Fin. We should have believed you but . . . you know, you were waving that knife."

Miles looked at Jeff with alarm. "Well, she was," said Jeff quietly.

It turns out that they hadn't found anyone to re-place me yet and Marc was hurling French insults at them daily because he had to pick up the slack. They wanted me back. They actually needed me.

"When can you start?" asked Miles.

"Today would be good," added Jeff.

"How about tomorrow?" I asked.

"Fine, tomorrow then."

"And you know what?" said Miles. "That raise you were asking for? I think it's time you got it."

Jeff glared at Miles.

I beamed as I walked out of the dining room and out the front door of the Heron. I felt like skipping as I started back up the highway toward home.

When I arrived home my mom was drinking tea and eating toast with blackberry jam on it.

"That smells good," I said.

"I'll make you some." She started to get up.

"Mom, relax. I'm fine." I put the kettle on and sliced the bread and put it in the toaster.

"By the way, I got my job back."

"Oh, honey! That's wonderful." She got up and kissed me on the forehead.

"I'm so proud of you." She smoothed my hair. "You know, I think I like it short like this."

Rocket curled up at my feet and sighed heavily.

My mom and I sat at the table together, talking, eating toast, sipping tea. If a stranger had looked in the window at that moment they would see a mom and her daughter, enjoying each other's company.

Every Tuesday my mom drove me back to the city to see Dr. Lundgren. She said she didn't mind. She visited art museums and galleries while she waited. At the end of my appointment one afternoon, Dr. Lundgren handed me a card with a phone number on it.

"This is completely against the rules, but Mr. Black sees you come out of my office every Tuesday and he's asked me all about you. I'm not allowed to talk about you, but I told him I'd give you his number and then you can decide if you want to talk to him yourself. I will add that he's eager to hear from you."

"Is his name really Mr. Black?"

"No. It's Cole. I don't think it's against the rules to tell you that."

I took the card with Cole's number on it and slipped it into my pocket.

THIRTY
SIX

Cole calls me "Madam George" now. Last week he taught me how to ride the bus. He sat next to me and held my hand. He drummed the fingers of his free hand on the seat next to him. Cole is a drummer in a band, a Dr. Seuss tribute band called Red Fish, Blue Fish. The truth is I'm half in love with him already.

"Fifty-seven blocks to go," he said, looking out the bus window.

As we passed through the Western Addition and then the Upper Richmond, I looked out at all the bustling Chinese and Russian restaurants and businesses.

"Thirty-one blocks." He tapped away.

The bus glided through the Sunset District. People got off, people got on.

Cole wasn't shy about telling me his story; years of therapy does that to people, I think. He told me everything the first time we talked on the phone. He spoke in a clipped staccato.

"My dad died from being kicked in the head. The official cause of death was an epidural hemorrhage. He was schizophrenic like me. I got it from him. He took off and left my mom and me when I was six. He started living under a freeway overpass. He was self-medicating and he was violent. One night he got in a fight with another homeless guy. That was it for him. My mom didn't tell me the real story till I was fifteen. Even after I was diagnosed I didn't believe I had it. I got caught up in tangent universe stuff, time travel, wormholes. I thought that I had telekinetic powers. Then I thought I was being watched by people who knew I was on to something important. Everywhere I went I saw this guy in a suit. I knew that he was following me. I thought he was a secret operative who worked for the government. I started building a surveillance-proof structure in our backyard where I could do my work without the government spying on me. Long story short, after four doctors, my mom found Dr. Lundgren. There was no way in hell she was watching me go the way my dad went.

I started feeling better. I shut down my work and I moved a drum kit out to the anti-surveillance shed."

"What about the guy who was following you?"

"He lives two doors down from us. His name is Norm. He sells insurance and he drives a blue Prius."

I laughed.

"Now you," said Cole. "Tell me all your sordid details."

So I did.

The bus stopped at the Cliff House at the very end of Geary where it meets the Great Highway. Cole took my hand and we got off the bus together.

In False Bay, Fin's story is one of those tales that will be around for a long time to come. In a strange way, it brought our little town closer together. Every one of us was seduced by Fin, every one of us fell a little bit in love with him, and it was hard not to talk about it. People shook their heads and remarked that it was *a helluva thing*. They wondered aloud at how such a charmer, such a people person, could actually be a psychopath. Well, I may not know the answer to that question but I know a thing or two about going off the deep end. Loss can do some pretty crazy things to people's heads.

My own life will always be a struggle, but it's one I'm better prepared for. Dr. Lundgren says these meds might not always work as well as they're working now. But right now I feel hopeful.

Right now I feel Lucky.

AUTHOR'S NOTE

Schizophrenia is a brain disorder that disrupts thinking and causes people to interpret reality abnormally. It affects about 1 percent of Americans. There isn't any single cause; genetics and environmental triggers are both factors. The severity of schizophrenia varies from person to person. Too often, those affected go without treatment. While there isn't a cure, schizophrenia can be managed with proper care from a licensed professional.

The media tend to link mental illnesses with criminal violence, but most people with schizophrenia are not violent toward others; they are more likely to be withdrawn and to prefer to be left alone. Efforts to destigmatize mental illness have made slow but steady progress. Sharing stories and experiences can help those with schizophrenia seek the care they need.

For more information about schizophrenia:

Read:
Me, Myself, and Them: A Firsthand Account of One Young Person's Experience with Schizophrenia, by Kurt Snyder, with Raquel E. Gur and Linda Wasmer Andrews, published by Oxford University Press in the Adolescent Mental Health Initiative series (2007).

Visit:
National Alliance on Mental Illness. "Schizophrenia." www.nami.org/Schizophrenia.

Band Back Together, a nonprofit support group. "Schizophrenia Resources." www.bandbacktogether.com/schizophrenia-resources.

The Intervoice (International Network for Training, Education, and Research into Hearing Voices). www.intervoiceonline.org.

Watch:
TED Talks by Elyn Saks, Orrin B. Evans Professor of Law, Psychology, and Psychiatry and the Behavioral Sciences at the University of Southern California, and psychologist Eleanor Longden—both of whom have been diagnosed with schizophrenia. www.ted.com/talks.

ACKNOWLEDGMENTS

Sincere thanks to the people who gave so generously of their time, knowledge, patience, encouragement, wisdom, music, and love to help me find my way through the trees to a clearing where I could tell this story. They are: Charlotte Sheedy, Elise Howard, Rachel Abrams, Meredith Kaffel, Mackenzie Brady, Krestyna Lypen, David Lidz, Alex Green, Malc McGookin, Martine McDonagh, Andrew Smith, Dr. Robert Levin, Ally Sheedy, David Prinz, and Django Reinhardt.